THE ADVENTUROUS FOUR

SHIPWRECKED!

THE ADVENTUROUS FOUR

SHIPWRECKED!

by

ENID BLYTON

Illustrated by Gavin Rowe

AWARD PUBLICATIONS LIMITED

For further information on Enid Blyton please visit *www.blyton.com*

ISBN 978-1-84135-734-8

This edition published by permission of Chorion Rights Limited

First published 1947 by Newnes as *The Adventurous Four*
First published by Award Publications Limited 2003
This edition first published 2009

Published by Award Publications Limited,
The Old Riding School, The Welbeck Estate,
Worksop, Nottinghamshire, S80 3LR

10 2

Printed in the United Kingdom

CONTENTS

CHAPTER ONE

The Beginning of the Adventures

Three children ran down a rocky path to the seashore. Tom went first, a small, wiry boy of twelve, his red hair gleaming in the sun. He looked round at the two girls following, and his green eyes twinkled.

"Want any help, you two?"

Zoe laughed in scorn. "Don't be so silly, Tom," she said.

"We're as good as you any day at running over the rocks," Pippa added.

The girls were twins, and very like each other, with thick golden plaits and deep blue eyes. They often laughed at Tom, and said he should have been called Carrots or Ginger or Marmalade, because of his red hair.

They were all on holiday, staying with their mother in a fishing village on the north-east coast of Scotland. Their father was away in the Air Force.

They had one great friend – Andy, who was fourteen. Andy was dark-haired and blue-eyed and knew everything about the sea, boats, and fishing. He could mimic any seabird, and could call the wild gulls to him by crying to them.

Andy liked the three children very much, and often took them out in his little boat. He had taught them all to swim like fishes, to row strongly, and to climb the rocky cliffs like cats.

Andy was sitting on the side of his little boat and grinning at the three children as they ran down the rocky path.

"Andy, did you ask your father what we wanted you to do?" said Tom.

"Yes, and he said yes," said Andy.

"Andy! How lovely!" said Pippa in excitement. "I never thought he'd lend you his boat so that we could all go on a trip to Little Island!"

"I was pretty surprised, too," said Andy. "But he knows I can handle the boat just as well as he can. We'll take plenty of food with us, and spend two days and a night on Little Island – and I'll show you where some weird birds nest, and the cove with yellow stones, and the cliff where about a million birds sit and call."

"Wow, it'll be brilliant!" said Tom, sitting up and hugging his knees. "No grown-ups. A little island with no one on it but ourselves. Too good to be true!"

They had always longed to visit the island that Andy had told them about but it was too far away to visit in a day. In great excitement the children made their plans.

"Let's take plenty of food," said Tom, who was always hungry. "I don't know why, but when I'm out on the sea I feel I could eat all the time."

"So do I," said Zoe. "It's crazy. I've never felt so hungry in my life as I have since we came here."

"Well, we'll get loads of food," said Tom. "And I'll bring my binoculars, so that we can see the birds well."

"And you'll bring warm clothes and rugs with you," said Andy.

"Oh, Andy! We won't need those, surely!" said Pippa. "This August is just about the hottest I've ever known."

"It's bound to break soon," said Andy. "And if it happens to turn cold while we're in the boat, you'll not like it."

"All right," said Tom. "We'll bring anything, so long as we can go. I say, what about that old wind-up record player in the shed? We could take that. Music sounds lovely on the water."

Andy was fond of music too, so he nodded.

On Thursday, the three children tired themselves out taking food, rugs, and other things down to the boat, which was quite a big one. It even had a little cabin to sit in, with a tiny table and stool, a bench and bunk. Nobody could stand in it, but that didn't matter.

Andy stared in astonishment at the amount of food. "Are you trying to feed an army?" he asked. "Six tins of soup – six tins of fruit – tins of corned beef – chocolate – condensed milk – biscuits – cocoa – sugar – and whatever's this?"

"Oh, that's tinned sausages," said Tom, going rather red. "Old Mrs MacPherson at the village shop said they were really good, so I bought some."

"Tom's nuts about sausages," said Pippa. "He'd like them for breakfast, lunch, and tea. Look, will these rugs be enough, Andy?"

"Yes," said Andy, looking at the odd collection of old rugs that Pippa had managed to get together. "Now, mind you all wear warm clothes too. Are you going to bring the record player, Tom? We can put it safely in the cabin, if you like."

Tom went back to get it, and some records. He also brought a tin of toffees and a camera.

"What time do we start, Andy?" asked Pippa.

"Be down here at half past six," said Andy. "I reckon we'll be at the island by about three in the afternoon then."

At six o'clock the next morning the three children were dressing hurriedly. It was a magnificent day. The eastern sky had been glowing red at dawn and was now pink and gold. The sun was already warm on their faces as they looked out of the little cottage window.

Their mother was awake. The children kissed her goodbye and ran down to the beach. Andy was already there, but to the children's surprise he looked rather serious.

"I don't think we should go," he said, as soon as he saw the children.

"Andy! Whatever do you mean?" they cried.

"Maybe you didn't see the sky this morning," said Andy. "It was as red as the geranium in our window. It was a really strange sky, and I reckon a storm will blow up today or tomorrow."

"Oh, don't be such a wet blanket, Andy," said Tom, climbing into the boat. "What does a storm matter? We'll be on the island before it comes, and if one comes tomorrow we can wait another day on the island. We've plenty of food."

"If my father hadn't gone out in my uncle's boat to fish, I think he'd stop us from going," said Andy, doubtfully. "But maybe the storm will blow off to the east. Get in, then, I'm glad to see you've got your jerseys on. If the wind blows up, we'll be cold tonight."

"Come on, Andy, push off," said Pippa. "I can't wait to go!"

It was a marvellous morning. The sea was full of sparkles and twinkles – it was blue and purple at a distance, clear green by

the boat. Zoe let her hand drag in the cool water. Pippa lay on her back in the boat, looking up at the cornflower-blue sky, feeling the boat bobbing up and down on the waves, and thinking she would love to stay like this for ever.

Tom was happy too. He loved sailing. He enjoyed thinking of his breakfast, and planned what he would have.

Only Andy was not happy. He wished his father had been there to advise him and he anxiously watched the sky for clouds. But there was not one to be seen.

"Now we're really off on our adventure," said Pippa. "There's no turning back now!"

But she didn't know what an extraordinary adventure it was going to be!

CHAPTER TWO

LOST IN THE STORM

As soon as the boat was clear of the bay Andy let the little brown sail billow out. The boat sped along.

"We go north-east," said Andy. "Can you steer by the sun, Tom?"

"Of course," said Tom. "And I can tell the time by it. I make it about half past seven."

"It's twenty past seven," said Pippa, looking at her watch. She whispered something to Zoe, who giggled.

"What are you giggling at?" asked Tom.

"Tell you in a minute," said Pippa. The boat flew on over the green water, and the spray whipped off the sea.

"Oh, am I hungry!" said Tom in half a minute. "What time are we going to have breakfast?"

The twins burst into squeals of laughter. "That's what we were whispering about just now!" said Pippa. "I said to Zoe, 'I bet the next thing Tom says will be that he's hungry and what about breakfast.' And sure enough, you did."

Tom laughed. "Well, I bet you feel the same," he said. "Why don't you see what we can have for breakfast?"

The girls went into the tiny cabin, which was crammed full of their food and other belongings. "What shall we have?" said Pippa. "What about pineapple chunks, and these hard-boiled eggs Mrs Andrews did for us yesterday evening, and some condensed milk, and chocolate?"

It was a most peculiar breakfast but the four children thought it was lovely. They had three loaves of bread with them, and some butter, and they dabbed the butter on to chunks of bread, took the eggs in their hand and bit first at the egg and then at the bread. Pippa put some salt wrapped in paper down on the deck for them to dip the eggs into.

"Idiot!" said Tom, as the wind promptly blew away paper, salt, and all. "As if the sea isn't salty enough already without adding more salt to it! Is there any more?"

There was some in a tin, and as this didn't blow away the children had plenty.

There was fresh water in a barrel, and everyone dipped in a cup and had a drink.

"That was a brilliant breakfast," said Tom. "I could do with it all over again."

The boat seemed to fly over the water. "We'll be at Little Island before three o'clock if we go on like this," said Andy.

"I'm so hot in the sun," said Pippa. "I wish I could be dragged behind the boat on a rope in the cool water."

The morning slid on. The sun rose higher and higher and at noon it was so hot that everyone put on sun-hats. The wind was still strong and whipped the tops from the waves as the boat flew along.

"It's past noon," said Tom. "What about . . ."

". . . some lunch!" chanted everyone, knowing exactly what Tom was going to say.

"I'm more thirsty than hungry," said Pippa. "What are you looking so worried about, Andy?"

"The weird colour the sky is getting over there," said Andy, nodding his head to the west.

They all looked.

"It's sort of coppery," said Tom.

"There's a storm blowing up," said Andy, sniffing the air like a dog. "I can smell it."

Andy always said he could smell a storm, and he was always right. The children looked anxiously towards the west.

"Shall we get to the island before it comes?" asked Pippa.

"We'll do our best," said Andy. "The little boat can't go faster than she's going now. As it is the sail is almost splitting with the wind!"

The sea turned a strange colour, a kind of blue-brown. "It's caused by the reflection of that funny sky," said Pippa, half nervous. "I say! It's weird being out here on the sea, miles away from land, with the sea and the sky doing odd things like this."

Then an even stranger thing happened. The wind, which had been blowing very strongly indeed, dropped completely. One moment it was blowing the children's hair straight back, the next there was not a breath of air. The sea fell calm and oily. The little fishing boat stopped running before the wind, and rode silently over the waves as if she were at anchor.

"That's odd," said Tom. "Not a bit of breeze now! Andy, we'll never get to the island if we don't get some wind. Shall we row?"

"No," said Andy, his face rather pale under its dark tan. "No, Tom. You'll get plenty of wind in a minute – more than we want. We must take in some of the sail. The ship will heel right over if we let her have all this sail when next the wind gets up. There's going to be a gale. I can hear it coming."

There was a bizarre humming noise in the air that seemed to come from nowhere at all. Then an enormous purple cloud blew up from the west and completely covered the sun. The sky went dark, and great spots of rain fell.

"It's coming now," said Andy. "Help me with the sail, Tom. Take the tiller, Pippa. Keep her heading the way we've been going. Pull, Tom, pull."

They pulled at the little brown sail, but before they had finished the storm broke. A great crash of thunder came from the purple cloud, and a flash of lightning split the sky in half.

And then the gale came. Tom and the girls had never, never imagined there could be such a wind. They could not hear themselves speak unless they shouted. Andy yelled to the girls:

"Get down into the cabin, quick, and shut the door and stay there."

"Can't we stay here?" cried Pippa. But Andy looked so stern and commanding that they did not dare to disobey. They almost fell into the cabin and shut the door. Outside, the wind seemed to get a voice – a voice that howled and wailed and lashed the sea into enormous waves that sent the little boat half over every time. Tins and everything else began to fall about. The girls picked them up and put them where they could not fall.

There was a crash as the bag of records fell down.

"Oh no!" cried Pippa. "They'll all be broken!"

Unfortunately they were – all but one. It was very sad. The girls carefully put the sole surviving record into a safe place and wondered what the boys would say when they knew. But it couldn't be helped.

Up above, on the deck, the two boys struggled with the wind and the sea. Tom wished he had an extra jersey and he shivered as wave after wave splashed on him, and the wind whipped by.

The deck was wet and slippery. The dark-green waves raced by, and the boat climbed up one steep wave after another,

and slid down the other side, only to climb up another enormous wave again.

Up and down, up and down she went, while Andy struggled with the sail.

"What are you trying to do?" yelled Tom, who was back at the tiller.

"Take in all the sail," shouted back Andy. "We can't go on like this. We'll be over."

But he didn't need to bother, for suddenly the sail ripped itself off the mast, flapped wildly for a second and then sped away into the sky. It was gone! Only a little rag was left, wriggling madly in the wind. The boat slowed down at once, for it no longer had the sail to take it along. But even the little rag of sail that was left was enough to take it a good speed over the waves.

Andy said nothing. He took the tiller with Tom, and together the boys faced the storm. Thunder rolled around and crashed in the skies. Lightning flickered and lit up the vast heaving waste of grey black sea. Stinging rain fell every now and again, and the boys bent their heads to it and shut their eyes. The wind lashed them and the spray whipped them. If this was an adventure, there was a great deal too much of it!

"Do you think we'll be all right, Andy?" shouted Tom. "Are we near the island?"

"I reckon we've passed it!" yelled back Andy. "At the rate we've been going we'd have been there by now. Goodness knows where we are now!"

Tom stared at Andy in silence. Past the island! A storm behind them! No sail! Whatever were they going to do?

CHAPTER THREE

SHIPWRECK!

For a long time the boat went on and on, its little rag of sail still flapping. Tom thought that the sail itself must have reached the great dark cloud that still covered the sky, the wind was so strong.

"I should think this wind's almost a hurricane, isn't it?" yelled Tom.

"Pretty near," shouted Andy. "But it's blowing itself out now."

Sure enough it was. Every now and again there was a lull when the wind dropped to a stiff breeze. Then it would blow again, furiously. The thunder was no longer overhead, but far off to the east. The lightning shimmered now and again, but did not light up the sea with the fierce brilliance it had two or three hours back.

Then, just as suddenly as it had come, the storm flew off. A sheet of bright blue sky appeared in the west, and swiftly grew bigger as the great cloud flew to the east. The world grew light again. The rain stopped. The wind died down to a breeze, and the boat no longer seemed to climb up and down steep hills.

The cabin door opened, and two green faces looked out sadly. "We've felt horribly seasick down here," said Pippa. "It was dreadful."

"What a terrible storm!" said Zoe. "Are we nearly at the island?"

"We've passed it, Andy says," said Tom gloomily. "We don't know where we are."

"Oh no! Look, the sail's gone!" said Zoe, shocked. "What *are* we to do for a sail?"

"There's an old one down in the cabin," said Andy. "Fetch it, will you, and I'll see if I can do something with it."

The sun shone down again. It was gloriously hot. Poor Tom, who had been chilled to the bone, loved it. He stripped off his wet shirt and put on his jersey. Ah, that was better!

Andy did not seem to feel either cold or wet. He took the old sail that the girls had found and had a good look at it. He thought he could rig it, with Tom's help. They must have a sail of some sort to get anywhere.

"I've heard my father say there are some desolate, rocky islands up away to the north of Little Island," said Andy, his wet jersey steaming in the hot sunshine. "We'll make for those. Maybe there will be someone there, or we could signal to a ship for help. I don't reckon we're going to get home too easily now."

At last Andy and Tom got the sail up and it flew in the breeze. Andy headed due north. It was about five o'clock now, and all the children were very hungry.

Pippa and Zoe had forgotten their sea-sickness and went below to get some food. Soon they were all eating heartily, and felt much better. They drank all the water before Andy knew there was none left.

"We shouldn't have done that," he said. "If we don't strike these islands I'm thinking of, we'll have no water tomorrow. Leave those apples, Zoe. We might be glad of the juice in the morning."

Zoe had been about to bite into a juicy apple, but she hastily put it down. In silence she and Pippa packed the apples away carefully in the cabin. Both the girls felt worried. Whatever would their mother have been thinking when that terrible storm blew up? They wished they were safely back at home.

The boat sailed on to the north. The sun slipped low into the west, and the boat's shadow lay purple on the sea. It was a beautiful evening.

"Look – gulls!" said Andy at last. "Maybe we're nearing land. Can't see any, though. We'd better anchor for the night, I should think."

And then the children got a great shock. There was no anchor! Andy stared in horror. How could he possibly have forgotten that his father had warned him to take the old anchor because he was lending Andy's uncle his own? How could he have forgotten? Now they couldn't anchor their boat. Now they would have to sail on until they came to land – and in the night they might strike a rock!

Andy stared over the restless sea in dismay. Well, there was nothing for it but to hope for the best. One of them must be at the helm all night long. It would be a moonlit night if only the sky was not clouded. Perhaps they would be lucky and sight land.

Pippa and Zoe were tired out. Andy ordered them to go below and rest. “You’d better go too, Tom,” he said. “You’ll have to come up and take your turn on deck tonight, and you’d better get a nap while you can.”

“But I don’t want to,” said Tom. “I can keep awake all right.”

“Go below, Tom,” said Andy, in the kind of voice that had to be obeyed. Tom went into the little cabin with the girls. They left the door open, for it was warm. The girls lay on the bunk and Tom curled up on the pile of rugs on the floor. In two minutes he was asleep. He did not know how tired he was. The wind, rain and sea had taken all his strength out of him for a time.

Andy stayed alone on deck. The little boat drove on and on. Andy hoped desperately that land would soon come in sight. He remembered so clearly what his father had said. Right past the Little Island, far to the north, lay other islands, desolate now, but once owned by a few farmers, who tried to get a hard living from the rocky soil. If only they could get help there!

Night fell darkly on the waters. The moon sailed into the sky, but clouds kept hiding her light. First the sea was gleaming silver, then it was black, then it was silver again. Andy wished he could see something besides the sea. But there was nothing.

The boy stayed on deck until midnight. He felt the night wind and wrapped a rug round his shoulders, though he did not feel really cold. After a while he whistled to Tom.

Tom awoke. "Coming," he said sleepily, and went up on deck. He shivered and Andy threw the rug round him. "Keep her heading straight," he said. "Give me a call if you see anything."

It was a curious experience up on deck all alone. The old sail flapped and creaked a little. The water splashed against the sides of the boat. The moon sailed in and out of the clouds until there came a thick mass of clouds which hid the moon altogether. Tom couldn't see anything at all. He strained his eyes to try and pierce through the darkness but except for the gleaming white top of a nearby wave now and then, he could see nothing. But he could hear something, quite suddenly. It sounded like crashing waves.

Tom longed for the moon to come out – and as he wished for it, it came sliding out from a cloud for a second before it disappeared again.

And in that tiny space of time Tom saw something that gave him a shock. The seas was breaking over big rocks just ahead!

"Andy! Andy!" yelled Tom, wrenching the tiller round. "Rocks ahead!"

Andy came stumbling up the steps, wide awake at once. He heard the sound of breaking waves and knew at once there were rocks ahead. He grabbed the tiller.

And then there came a grating noise and a long groan from the boat. She was on the rocks! She had run straight on to them – and there she lay, groaning, half over, slanting so much that the girls in the little cabin were thrown out of the bunk.

"Hold on, Tom," shouted Andy, clutching at Tom, who seemed about to slide overboard. "Hold on! She's settling!"

The boat did settle. She seemed to be wedged between two rocks that were holding her tightly, all on the slant. Waves splashed over one side of her deck.

For a few minutes the children hardly dared to breathe – and then Andy spoke.

"She's fast," he said. "She may have a hole in her bottom, but she won't sink while she's held like this. We must wait till dawn."

So they waited, clinging uncomfortably to the slanting sides of the ship. Dawn was not far off. It silvered the eastern sky as they waited. The light grew stronger, and then a gold edge appeared on the horizon. The sun was about to rise.

And in the golden light of the early sun they saw something not far off that made them shout for joy.

"Land ho!" they yelled, and would have danced in delight if only the deck had not been so slanting.

A sandy shore stretched to a rocky cliff. Stunted trees grew further inland, touched with gold by the rising sun. It was an island of some sort, desolate, rocky and lonely – but it was at least land! Somewhere where they could light a fire to make themselves warm. Somewhere where other people might be to give them a helping hand.

"We'll have to swim for it," said Andy. "It's not very far. Once we're clear of these rocks we'll be all right. In fact, now that the tide has gone down a bit we could almost walk over the rocks to the shallow water that runs up the shore."

Half wading, half swimming, they made their way over and between the reef of rocks, and paddled to shore. The sun began

to warm their cold bodies. How glad they all were that they had taken Andy's advice and put on warm clothes!

"Well," said Andy, when they had reached the shore, "we'll climb up these cliffs, and see if we can spot any houses."

They climbed the rocky cliffs. When they got to the top they looked around. A small stunted wood grew a little way off, on a hillside. Low bushes crouched here and there as if to hide from the strong wind that blew always across the island. Grass crept over the rocky earth, and a few daisies flowered. But there were no signs of any houses, or of any human beings.

Andy made up his mind quickly.

"If we've got to be stranded here for a time we *must* get everything out of our boat," he said. "Thank goodness we've got a certain amount of food and some rugs. We can do it now while the tide is at its lowest. When it's high it will completely cover the deck. Come on, Tom. You girls can stand halfway to the boat in that shallow water, and we'll carry things to you over the rocks. Then you can take them back to the shore. It will be better than us all scrambling about on the rocks and dropping everything."

And so they began to empty the boat of all it held – food, rugs, record player, camera, binoculars, stool, tables, tools, crockery, kettle, matches, little stove, everything! It took a long time, but before they had finished the tide had risen and the decks were awash. The cabin was full of water!

"We can't do anything more," said Andy. "Let's go and have a rest, and something to eat. I'm starving."

CHAPTER FOUR

On the Unknown Island

It was a rather solemn set of children who sat down on the shore to eat breakfast. They had been brave during the storm, but now they all felt very tired and rather scared. It was strange to think they might have to stay for quite a long time on the unknown island until they were rescued – and supposing they were right off the route of the ships and steamers that used those seas?

Andy took charge. He stared out at their wrecked boat, and wrinkled his forehead.

"Well, we're in a nice fix," he said. "But we'll forget it for a minute and enjoy our breakfast. We'd better finish up all the bread, for it'll soon be stale. We'll eat all the food that might go bad. And what about something hot to drink? I don't feel really cold, but it would do us good to get something hot inside us. Look, I brought the matches with me, wrapped in this oilskin so that they wouldn't get wet. We can't get the stove going till we get the can of paraffin out of the locker in the boat – we forgot that – so we'd better make a fire on the beach."

Tom and Pippa collected sticks, and soon there was a fine fire going. Andy filled the kettle from a stream he found running down the little hill in the distance.

"Good, the fire's going well," he said. "Where's the tin of cocoa?"

The kettle soon boiled, and the children made thick cocoa. They added tinned milk to it and drank with enjoyment. The twins, who were cold, felt warmed up at once.

Tom yawned. He was not used to keeping awake half the night. The girls were tired out, too, for they had been very seasick in the storm.

Andy had laid out the rugs in the sun. Now he felt them, and found that they were almost dry.

"We'd better get off our wet things and hang them on the bushes to dry," he said. "We'll roll ourselves in these rugs and lie down in the sheltered corner over there by the cliff, and sleep off our bad night."

So in three or four minutes all that could be seen of the children were four tightly-rolled bundles lying peacefully asleep in the sunshine. Their damp clothes, spread out on bushes to dry, were already steaming in the heat.

Andy woke first. He threw off his rug and went to feel his clothes on the bush. They were perfectly dry. He put them on, and then went to the big pile of things they had taken from the boat. He looked among them and found a fishing-line.

He hunted about for a sandworm, baited his hook, and clambered out on the rocks, where deep water swirled around him. He lowered his line into the water. In ten minutes he had caught his first fish, and was baiting the line again.

Tom awoke next and woke the girls up. They put on their warm clothes and waved to Andy.

"Andy's getting our lunch!" said Pippa. "I suppose you're feeling as hungry as usual, Tom?"

"I could eat a whale!" said Tom.

It was fun cooking the fish over a fire. It smelled delicious. There was no bread left

so the children had to eat the fish by itself, but they were so hungry that they didn't mind at all.

"It's about two o'clock in the afternoon," said Andy, looking at the sun. "Now, the first thing to do is to find a good place to sleep for the night. Then we'd better explore the island, if we've time. The food we've got with us won't last a great while, but at any rate we can always get fish, and I expect we'll find some berries we can eat, too."

He stood up and looked all round the cliff.

"I wonder if there's a cave we could sleep in at night," he said. But there didn't seem to be any caves at all, though the children hunted carefully all along the cliff.

"How will anyone know we are here?" asked Pippa. "We should put up some sort of a sign, shouldn't we, to show any passing ship or steamer that we are here?"

"Yes," said Andy. "I've been thinking about that. I'll take down the old sail, and we'll tie it to a tree on the top of the cliff. That will make a great signal."

"Good idea!" said Tom. "It'll flap in the wind and be seen for miles."

"We'll find a sleeping place for the night before we do that," said Andy. "It looks like rain again now – see that low cloud over there? We don't want to be soaked in our sleep. Come on."

They left the sandy cove and climbed up the steep cliff. It was hard going, but they got to the top at last and once more looked across the island. They could not see right across it because the hill in the middle stopped their view, so they did not know how big or small it was. All they knew was that, at present, they could not see any sign of anyone else there or of any house or other building.

"Let's make our way to the hill," said Andy, anxious to get on. "There's bracken there, and heather, and maybe we can find a hill-cave to snuggle in. Bracken and heather make a fine bed, and we've got the rugs for covers."

They ran to the hill. It had a little wood of wind-blown pines and birches, but there was no cave in the hillside they could shelter in. It was covered with thick-growing bracken and heather, with a few stunted gorse bushes – but there was no place that would really give them a safe shelter to sleep.

"Well, we'll have to rig up a tent of some sort," said Andy at last. "I'm not going to be soaked through tonight. I've had enough of that to last me for quite a while."

"A tent, Andy?" said Tom. "Wherever would we get a tent from?"

"I'm going to get the old sail off the boat," said Andy. "We can use it for a signal by day and a tent by night. It's big enough to cover us all quite well."

"Andy, you *have* got good ideas!" said

Pippa. "I should never have thought of that. Well, shall we go back then and help you?"

"No," said Andy. "You stay here with Tom and help him to build a kind of tent-house that we can just drape the sail over. You'll want some stout branches, stuck well into the ground. I'll go and get the sail."

Andy went off down to the shore again, and clambered and waded out to the boat. He was soon taking down the old sail.

The others hunted for good branches. The ones lying on the ground were too brittle and old, they found.

"These'll only be good for firewood," said Tom. "We'll have to break a few growing branches off the trees."

It was difficult to do this, but they managed it at last. Then they drove the stout sticks into the heathery ground and made a kind of circle with them, big enough to hold them all.

They had just finished when Andy came back, bent double under the heavy sail. He threw it down and panted.

"I thought I'd never get it up the cliff," he said. "Hey, those walls look good. The sail will go over them nicely."

Eight willing hands helped to arrange the brown sail over the circle of sticks stuck firmly into the ground. The weight of the sail kept it down, and when the children had finished, they had made a kind of round brown tent, with no doorway. But as the children could get in anywhere under the tent simply by lifting up the sail, it didn't matter having no doorway.

"We'll gather a nice pile of heather and put it inside the tent to lie on," said Tom. "And with our rugs, too, we'll be as cosy and warm as toast!"

"There isn't time to explore the island now," said Andy, looking in surprise at the sinking sun. "We've taken ages over the tent. We'll go all over the island tomorrow."

"I can't wait," said Zoe. "I wonder what we'll find!"

CHAPTER FIVE

Making the Best of Things

The children were all hungry again. Andy thought it would be better to bring everything up from the shore, and put it near their tent.

"We may have to make our tent a sort of home," he said. "We don't want to have to keep climbing up and down that rocky cliff every time we want a cup or a kettle! Anyhow, we're quite near the spring here, and we can easily get water whenever we want to."

So for the next hour or so the children fetched all their belongings. Some of them were very difficult to get up the cliff. The record player was almost impossible till Andy thought of the idea of tying a rope round it and hauling it gently up by that.

"Oh no! Are all the records broken?" said Tom in dismay, as he picked up the cracked records.

"Yes, they fell and broke during that terrible storm," said Pippa. "Leave them behind. They're no use. There's just one that's not broken – now, where is it?"

They found it at last and looked at it.

"What a pity! This is a silly record – it *would* be the only one that's left unbroken!" said Zoe. "On one side it's a girl singing a kind of lullaby, without even any music, and on the other it's nursery rhymes. The silliest one we've got!"

"Oh well, bring it along," said Tom. "And where's my camera? It doesn't look as if I'll find any good pictures to take, but I may as well have it."

By the time they had got everything to the tent they were really very tired. They cooked the rest of the fish and opened a tin of peaches. They ate an apple each, broke a bar of chocolate into four pieces, and then drank some hot cocoa. It was a good meal and they enjoyed it. The sun was now almost gone and the first star was shining brightly.

"Well, we've had an adventurous day," said Pippa, yawning. "I slept all the morning, but I feel really sleepy again already."

"Come on," said Andy. "We want more heather for our beds. Tom, stamp out the fire. We don't want to set the hill alight, and the heather is very dry."

Tom stamped out the fire. The girls filled the tent with more heather. Andy took the largest rug and spread it all over the springy pile.

"You girls can sleep on this side of the tent, and Tom and I will take the other," he said. "There are plenty of rugs, luckily."

Nobody undressed. Life seemed quite different on an unknown island. And nobody even *thought* of washing!

They rolled themselves up in their rugs and lay flat on the heathery bed. It was beautifully soft and springy, and very comfortable once they had pressed down several sharp bits that stuck into them.

Tom was asleep at once. The girls lay awake for a minute or two. Pippa felt very hot, for the tent was airless, and the four of them made quite a crowd in it. Andy raised one side of the sail and let the breeze in. It was lovely, for now the girls could see out.

The moonlight lay on the hillside and everything was clear till the clouds sailed across the moon. Andy lay awake, leaning on his elbow, looking out down the hillside, and listening to the sound of the waves in the distance, under the cliff.

"We must certainly hang out a signal every day," he thought. "It might be seen by some passing ship. We must find a better place to live in too, for if the weather should break up, this tent won't be any use. And I wonder if it's possible to get the boat off the rocks and patch her up. If we could do that, maybe we might have a shot at sailing home."

All the children slept soundly that night and didn't wake until the sun was fairly high – about eight o'clock in the morning. Andy as usual woke first and rolled out of the tent quietly. But he had woken Tom, and when the boy yawned loudly the girls woke too.

It was a fine sunny morning with clouds scudding across the sky. The first thing, of course, was breakfast – but it had to be caught! So the boys went fishing and the girls managed to catch about twenty large prawns in a pool on the sandy shore. They cooked their catch and ate hungrily.

"I really feel dirty," said Pippa. "I'm going to wash at the spring. Are you coming, Zoe?"

"Yes," said Zoe. "And I vote we all have a swim today. That'll clean us up a bit too."

They all felt cleaner after a rinse and splash in the spring. Tom and Andy made the fixing of the signal their next job. They found a good tree – at least, it was a good one for their purpose, for it had been struck by lightning at one time and now stood straight and bare on the top of the cliff.

It took the two boys about an hour to climb the tree and fix the sail-signal. It flapped out well in the breeze and Andy was sure it could be seen from a great distance. They climbed down again and went back to the girls.

"What about exploring the island now?" asked Tom. "I feel just like a good walk!"

"Well, the island may be too small for a good walk!" said Andy. "We'll see. Ready, you girls?"

They were all ready for their walk. First they climbed the hill and stood on the top, looking to see what they could spy.

From the top of the hill they could see

all around their island and certainly it was not very big – only about a mile and a half long and about a mile wide. They could see the blue water all around it.

But not far off were other islands! They lay in the sea, blue and misty in the distance. But as far as the children could see, there were no houses or buildings of any kind on them. They seemed as desolate and lonely as their own island. The cries of seabirds came as they stood on the hill, and big white gulls swooped around them – but except for that sound, and the far-off splash of waves, there was no other sound to be heard. No shout, no hoot of a horn, no drone of an aeroplane. They might be lost in the very middle of the ocean for all they could see or hear!

"I don't believe a single soul lives on these islands," said Andy, his face rather grave. "Come on, let's go down to this side of the hill. We may as well find out all there is to know."

As they went down the hill and came to the level ground again, Tom stopped in astonishment. "Look!" he said. "Potato plants!"

The children looked, and sure enough, growing completely wild around them were plants that looked exactly like potatoes! Andy pulled one up – and there, clinging to the roots, were a dozen or more small white potatoes!

"That's strange!" said Andy, staring round. "At some time or other there must have been people living here, and they grew potatoes. Some have seeded themselves and grown wild. But the thing is, *if* people lived here, where did they live? They must have lived somewhere!"

"How odd," said Tom, looking all round as if he expected houses to spring from the ground.

And then Pippa gave a shout. "I believe I can see the chimney of a house! Look! Where the ground dips down suddenly over there."

The others looked. They saw that the ground did suddenly dip down into a kind of hollow, well protected from the wind – just the place where people might build a house. They tore over the rocky ground to the dip, expecting they hardly knew what.

And what a surprise they got when at last they reached the hollow and looked down into it!

CHAPTER SIX

A Strange Little Home

The four children stood at the top of the steep dip. The hollow ran right down to the sea – and in it was a cluster of small buildings!

But what strange buildings! The roofs were off, the chimneys were gone – all but the one they had seen – the walls were fallen in, and everything looked forlorn and deserted.

"Nothing but ruins!" said Tom, in astonishment. "Whatever happened to make the houses and sheds fall to pieces like that?"

"I think I know," said Andy. "A year or two ago there came a great storm to these parts, so great that the people of our village fled inshore for miles, because the sea battered our houses and flooded our streets. The storm must have been even worse on these unprotected islands here, and I should think the sea came into this hollow and battered the farm to bits! Look at that chimney-stack there, all black and broken – that was struck by lightning, I should think."

The four children gazed down at the poor, hollow house and out-buildings. A little farm had once been there, a poor farm maybe, trying to grow a few potatoes in the rocky ground, to keep a few goats or cows, and to take from the sea enough fish to live on.

Now the folk had all gone, unable to battle with the great sea-storms that swept over their farm and destroyed their living.

"This explains the potatoes," said Pippa. "That stretch of struggling potato plants must once have been a field."

"Let's go down into the hollow and have a look round," said Andy. So down into the dip they scrambled and wandered round the ruined buildings. Nothing had been left – all the furniture had been taken away, and even the gates and doors removed. Seashore weeds grew up from the floors of the farmhouse.

At last they came to a little wooden

shack where perhaps a cow or two had been kept in the winter. For some reason it had escaped being beaten in by the waves and still stood upright, its one window broken and its floor covered with a creeping weed.

Andy looked at it carefully. "This wouldn't be a bad place to make into a little house for ourselves," he said. "I was thinking we'd have to try and build one somehow, but this will do if we patch it up a bit. The sail won't be any use at all if the weather breaks up, and also it's going to be a great nuisance to keep taking it down from the signal-tree each night for our tent and putting it back again in the mornings."

"Oh yes!" said Tom in delight. "Let's make this our house! That would be fun. Then we could leave the sail flapping for our signal all the time."

They all went into the shack. It was not very large, more like a big bicycle shed, though the roof was higher. A wooden partition divided it into two.

"We'll take that down," said Andy. "It would be better to have one fairly big room than two tiny ones."

"Well, we'd better start work at once, hadn't we?" said Tom eagerly. "We shall have to bring all our things here and make it a bit home-like. And all those weeds will have to be cleared."

"Yes, and we'll spread the floor with clean sand," said Pippa. "Listen, you boys clear up the weeds for us, and Zoe and I will go to that old potato field and find the biggest potatoes we can, and cook them in their jackets for lunch!"

"Good idea," said Tom, feeling hungry at once. "Come on, Andy, let's start cleaning up the place now. We can't do much till that's finished."

The two boys set to work. They pulled up the creeping weed in handfuls and piled it outside. They got tufts of stiff heather and, using them as brushes, swept the cobwebs from the walls and rough ceiling. Tom broke the remaining glass of the window, gathered the broken bits carefully together and tucked them into the bottom of the old rubbish-heap so that no one could be cut by a splinter.

Andy made a rough fireplace just outside the shack, with stones from the hearth of the ruined farmhouse.

"We can't have the fire inside because this shack has no chimney," he said, "and we'd be choked with the smoke. Anyway, I've made the fireplace out of the wind and we ought to be able to cook all right on it. Zoe, you can bake the potatoes there, once the stones get hot. Tom, get some sticks and start a fire."

Zoe and Pippa peeped inside the shack. It looked clean and tidy now, though very bare. The two girls had pulled plenty of good potatoes from the old, weedy field, and had washed them in the spring water. They would be fine, baked in their jackets, though it was a pity there was no butter left and no salt.

Tom fetched some clean sand from the shore and scattered it over the earth floor. It looked very neat and clean.

"We'll have to get heaps of heather and bracken in for beds again," said Pippa, "just as we did for our tent. We must bring the little table here, and the stool, and all the cups and things. It will make it seem like home."

They had potatoes and chocolate for lunch, with plenty of cold spring water. Tom could have eaten three times as much but he had to be content with five large potatoes and a whole bar of chocolate.

"We'll have fish tonight," promised Andy. "The water round about this island is just thick with fish. We'll always have plenty to eat so long as we don't get tired of fish! We'll hunt for shellfish too."

After their lunch the children separated. The girls were to go to the nearest patches of heather and bracken and bring in armfuls of it for beds. The boys were to make journeys to and from the tent, and bring in all their belongings.

"When the tide's down tonight I'll get the tin of paraffin out of the locker of the boat," said Andy. "That won't have been spoilt by the seawater because it's got a tight-fitting lid. We can cook over the stove then, as well as over a fire, if we want to."

The children were very busy that afternoon. Zoe and Pippa got enough heather and bracken to make two beds, one at each side of the shack. They piled the tough bracken on the floor first, and then the softer heather on top. Then they spread each bed with a rug, and put another rug, neatly folded up, to be used as a blanket at night.

The boys brought in the thick plain crockery. It was just right for the shack, but where was it to be put?

"We really can't keep it on the floor," said Zoe. "It'll get broken. I wish we had a shelf to put things on. It would give us much more room if only we could get these odd things out of the way."

Andy disappeared for a few minutes. When he came back he carried a wooden board. He grinned at the surprised children.

"I remembered seeing an old shelf in what must have been the kitchen of the farmhouse," he said. "So I went in and wrenched it down from the wall. Tom, where did you put the tools and the box of nails?"

"Down there by our bed," said Tom. Andy picked up a hammer and the box of nails. "Where do you want the shelf?" he asked the girls.

"Over there, at the back of the shack, just about shoulder-height," said Zoe. "What a lovely shelf that will make, Andy, it'll take everything!"

So it did! Once Andy had nailed it up, the girls arranged the crockery there, the kettle, one or two pans, the binoculars, camera and other things. The record player would not go on the shelf so they put it into a corner.

By this time the shack really looked

good! There were the two neat beds at the sides, the table in the middle, with the stool, the neatly-sanded floor, the shelf at the back with its array of goods! The children felt really pleased with it.

Andy filled the paraffin stove. "We could boil some potatoes tonight for a change," he said. "We've got a little saucepan, haven't we?"

"Yes," said Zoe. "I'll boil them and mash them, but they'll taste a bit odd without butter or salt. And we'll open another tin of fruit."

They had a most delicious supper and enjoyed every bit of it. They didn't even mind going without salt in the potatoes. They ate their supper sitting outside the open doorway of the shack, looking out to the evening sea. The gulls called high in the air, and the splash of the little white-edged waves came to them every now and again.

"Now we'll turn in!" said Andy with a yawn. "It will be fun to sleep in our little house for the first time! Come on, let's leave the washing-up till the morning. We're all tired out!"

CHAPTER SEVEN

A Strange Discovery

The next day the children went to make sure that their sail-signal was still safely tied to the signal-tree at the top of the cliff. It was. It flapped there steadily, a signal to any passing ship that there were people on the island who needed help.

"Suppose no help comes?" said Tom. "Will we have to stay here all winter?"

"Yes, unless you'd like to try to swim hundreds of miles back home!" said Andy.

The children looked at one another. Stay there for the winter! It was all very well having an adventure on an island for three or four days, but to stay there all the winter, in the bitter cold and raging storms, was not a pleasant thought.

"Don't look so gloomy," said Andy. "We may be rescued any day. I can't think that no ship ever passes these islands. After all, there were people living here not so long ago, and they must have had supplies from time to time, so ships must come by here sometimes. And maybe there are people living on one of the other islands. I think perhaps at very low tide we could cross to the next island by that line of rocks over there, and explore that. We may find dozens of people, for all we know!"

Everyone cheered up. Of course! There seemed to be five or six islands near to their own; people would surely be living on one or other of them, especially on the bigger ones.

The children thoroughly explored the little island again, but found nothing interesting at all. They could see that the farm-people had used the level stretch of land on the more southerly side of the island for their fields. In one place, Pippa found some runner-beans growing over a tangle of brambles, and she called out in excitement:

"Beans! We'll eat them for supper!"

The others came to look. "I expect these seeded themselves too," said Andy. "Maybe there was a bean-field just here. Well, we're not doing too badly, with potatoes and beans and fish for a meal!"

The tide was very low that evening. The children stood on a rocky ledge, looking to the north where the other islands lay, blue with a summery mist.

"I'd really like to go across those rocks tomorrow morning when the tide is low again," said Andy. "We could take food for the day, see what was on the next island, and climb back across the rocks at low tide tomorrow night."

"Yes, why not?" cried the twins, and Tom did a little war-dance on the rocky ledge in excitement. Who knew what they might find on the next island.

That night they cooked some potatoes in their skins, and let them go cold to take with them the next day.

"We'll cook the sausages that are in one of the tins, let them go cold, and take those, too," said Pippa. "We can catch some fish tomorrow night for our supper when we come home."

The next morning they ran to the rocks again.

"Come on!" said Andy. "We'd better go now, before the tide turns."

They jumped on to the rocks, and then began to make their way carefully over them. Soon they came to the end of them, and waded to the sandy shore of the next island.

"Now we're on island number two!" said Tom, leaping about. "Gosh, am I hungry!"

So was everyone. "Well, if we eat all our food now, we'll have to wait ages for our next meal, unless we can find something on this island," said Andy, but he was hungry too, so they ate their cold sausages and potatoes, and sucked a toffee each.

Then they set off to explore the second island. They turned to climb the cliffs – and had a big surprise!

"Look! Caves!" said Tom, pointing to big black openings in the cliff. "Look at that! Caves of all kinds and sizes and shapes! Let's have a look at them."

They made their way to the first cave, and just outside it Andy stopped and stared at something in the sand.

"What's up?" asked Tom.

"That!" said Andy, and he pointed to a cigarette-end that lay rolling a little in the breeze.

"A cigarette-end!" said Tom, looking all round, as if he were looking for the one who had smoked it. "Well! Somebody has been here all right, and not very long ago, either. But there's not a single house on this island, ruined or whole!"

"Perhaps the people live in these caves," said Pippa, looking half timidly at the first one.

"We'll go in and see," said Andy. He pulled a roll of oilskin from his pocket and out of it took a half-candle and a box of matches. Andy never ran any risk of his matches getting wet, and now the children were glad that he was so careful, for no one really wanted to go into the caves without a light of some sort.

Andy lit the candle and then stepped into the first cave. The others followed him. The floor was thick with silvery sand, and the walls were high and smooth. The cave ran back a long way, and narrowed into an archway. Through this the children went into another cave, the tiny light of the candle shining on rocky grey walls, and a high, rough roof. The floor of the cave then began to go upwards, and became rocky instead of sandy. The cave narrowed into a passage, the roof of which was at times so low that they bumped their heads against it.

And then they came to the Round Cave, which was the name they at once gave the last strange cave. It was almost perfectly round, and as the floor slanted down towards the middle, it felt like being inside a hollow ball!

But it wasn't the roundness of the cave that startled the four children, it was what it held!

Piled high everywhere were boxes, sacks, and big tin chests with strange words on them! Some piles reached to the roof of the cave, others reached halfway.

"Hey! Look at that!" said Tom, in utter amazement. "Whatever's in all those boxes and things, and why are they all stored here?"

The little flame of the candle flickered on the strange array in the cave. Andy set the candle gently down on a flat piece of rock, and pulled the neck of a thick brown sack undone. It was lined with coarse blue paper. He undid that, and then gave a low cry of surprise.

"Sugar! Stranger and stranger! I was expecting treasure or something – and it's sugar! I wonder what's in the other sacks and boxes."

Some the children could not force open, but others were already opened, as if someone had taken from them some of the contents. The boxes were full of tins – there were tins of soup, meat, vegetables, fruit, sardines – everything one could think of. There was a chest of flour, a chest of tea,

tins of salt, even tins of butter and lard, well-sealed and airtight.

"How did all these come here?" said Pippa in a puzzled voice. "And who do you suppose they belong to? As far as we know there isn't a single person on the island."

"I don't know," said Andy. "But we won't need to starve while there's all this food stored here!"

"But should we take it, if it belongs to someone else?" said Zoe, frightened.

"We can pay the person it belongs to," said Andy. "My father and your mother will gladly pay, to keep us from starving if we have to spend the winter here!"

"Well, come on then, let's take all we want," said Tom, feeling so hungry that he couldn't wait a minute longer. "We'll keep a careful account of everything we take, and pay the bill and a little more when we find out who owns this very curious store."

"You're right, Tom," said Andy, in a puzzled voice. "It is a *very* curious store!"

CHAPTER EIGHT

Odder and Odder

The children each chose what they thought they would like to take away and carried it down the narrow passages that led from the Round Cave to the shore-cave.

When they reached the open air Tom took a deep breath and set down his load. "My goodness, it was stuffy up there," he said.

"What puzzles me is why it wasn't more stuffy than it was," said Andy. "Air must get into that Round Cave through some hole we didn't see. Pick up your things, Tom, the tide's coming in. We can't stay on this beach. The sea will reach the cave before long."

"It's all right for about ten minutes," said Tom, pulling a fat little notebook from his pocket. "I just want to jot down a list of all the things we've taken, in case we eat them up and then forget what we had."

He wrote everything down, shut his notebook with a snap, and pushed it back into his pocket. Then he picked up his load and followed Andy up the steep, rocky path.

Until the tide went out that night the children were prisoners on the second island, for there was no way to get back to their own island except by the line of rocks. This was now completely covered by the tide, and great showers of spray were sent high into the air as the water crashed against the rocks over which they had clambered early that day.

"Anyone got a tin-opener?" asked Tom, his mouth watering at the sight of the labels on the tins.

Andy had. In Andy's pockets there was almost anything that anyone could possibly want, from tin-tacks to toffee.

They opened a tin of ham and had a great feast. But they felt very thirsty afterwards, and as they had not found any spring or stream on the second island they could not think what to do.

"Well, why don't we open a tin of pineapple?" said Tom at last. "The chunks will be lovely and juicy and we can all have a drink of the juice in the tin too."

So the pineapple was opened and both empty tins were carefully buried by the children. The gulls swooped round them all the time they ate, screaming loudly.

Andy imitated them and they grew even more excited, at last landing on the ground behind the children and waiting there almost within touch.

"These gulls know that where there are people, there may be food," said Andy. "But how do they know that? These islands seem quite bare and empty."

"And how did all that food come to be in the Round Cave?" said Pippa. "Could it have been there for years, do you suppose, and have been forgotten?"

"No," said Andy. "It hasn't been there very long. The sugar was still soft, and sugar goes hard if it is stored for long. That cigarette-end we found too – that had been smoked not less than a week or two ago, or the wind would have blown it into bits."

"Andy, don't you think it would be a good thing to stay on this island and live here, instead of going back to our own island?" asked Zoe. "We should be near to a good food supply then!"

"No, I don't," said Andy at once. "You forget we've left a signal on our island – and if any ship sees it and calls for us, we might be on this island, unable to be rescued because the tide was high and we couldn't get back."

"But couldn't we tie the signal up somewhere on this island?" said Tom.

"No," said Andy. "No ship could get to us here. This island is almost surrounded by a reef of the worst rocks I've ever seen. Look at them, right out there."

The children looked. Andy was right. A

jagged line of rocks ran some way out from the coast. Between the rocks and the coast the sea lay trapped in a kind of big lagoon or lake, calm and smooth.

Tom frowned and looked puzzled. "Well, if no ship can get in to rescue us if we stay on this island," he said, "how in the world did one get in to land all that food in the cave?"

Andy stared at Tom and looked as puzzled as Tom did. "Yes, that's odd," he said. "Well, maybe there is a way through at high tide. But we can't risk it. We must live on the first island, and when we want food we must come here and get it – and maybe we'll run into the folk who so strangely made the store in the Round Cave."

Zoe stood up and tried to see what the next island was like. It looked much bigger than the first two. There was no line of rocks stretching to it, only an unbroken spread of blue water. To get to the third island they would have to swim, or use a boat.

"Do you think we'd better leave a note in the cave to say that we are on the first island and would like to be rescued?" said

Tom. "The people may come back at any time, and we could go away in their boat."

Andy shook his head. "I think we won't leave a note, or anything else to show we've been here," he said. "There's something a bit mysterious about all this, and if there's a secret going on, we'd better keep out of it till we know what it is."

"Oh, Andy! Whatever do you mean?" cried Zoe.

"I don't *know* what I mean," said Andy. "It's just a feeling I have, that's all. Maybe I'm wrong, but one of us will come over here every day at low tide and just see if there's somebody about before we let them know we're here."

"But what about all our footmarks round the cave?" said Tom.

"The tide will wash all those right away," said Andy. "Look over the cliff-edge, Tom, you will see the tide has gone right into the cave now. There is absolutely nothing that will show we have been there."

"Except that some of the food is missing," said Zoe. "You've forgotten that, Andy."

"No, I haven't," said Andy. "There's so

much in that cave that I don't think anyone will miss the little we've taken. I don't expect it's checked at all. Nobody would think that any strangers would ever visit that cave."

The children wandered over the island and looked for bilberries, which were fruiting there in great numbers. The island was quite deserted. It did not look as if anyone had ever lived there at all.

The tide went down and the line of rocks began to show. The children clambered down to the shore to go back to their own island. They had tied to their backs the food they had taken, and Andy told everyone to be very careful.

"We don't want to lose our food in a deep pool!" he said. "So don't rush along too fast, Tom. You're always in such a hurry!"

The rocks were wet and slippery, but the children were very careful indeed. They got back to their little hut at last and all of them were delighted to see it. It really felt like coming home.

"It seems too early to go to bed," murmured Pippa sleepily. "But I can't keep awake another minute!"

And she fell asleep at once. So did Zoe. Tom lay down too. Andy sat up for a while, looking out towards the second island and wondering about a lot of things.

Then he too lay down and fell asleep – but not for long!

A strange and curious noise awoke him. It came into his dreams, startled him and roused him so that he sat up, puzzled and alarmed.

"Tom! Wake up!" said Andy. "Listen to that noise. What is it?"

Tom awoke and listened. "It's a motor-bike," he said, half asleep.

"Don't be so stupid!" said Andy. "A motor-bike on this island! You're dreaming. Come on, listen! There's a really strange noise."

The noise itself hummed away into silence. The gulls screamed but soon became quiet. Andy sat and listened a little longer and then, as no more noise came, lay down on his bed again.

"Odder and odder," said Andy to himself. "We seem to have come to some most mysterious islands – and I'm going to find out what's happening!"

CHAPTER NINE

THE MYSTERIOUS VISITORS

The next day the children talked about the strange noise that Andy had heard.

"I tell you, it sounded exactly like a motor-bike," Tom said firmly, and nothing would make him admit that it wasn't.

"It might be a motor-boat, perhaps!" said Pippa suddenly. The others stared at her. For some reason, nobody had thought of motor-boats till then.

"Yes, it could well have been!" said Andy. "But what's a motor-boat doing here? Well, anyway, it means that we can be rescued!"

"Of course!" said Tom. "Let's go and find the motor-boat. What a surprise they'll get when they suddenly see us! They'll wonder where on earth we've come from."

"Tom, don't be in such a hurry," said Andy, pulling the impatient boy down into the heather. "I think there's something funny going on here, and before we show ourselves we'd better find out if we'll be welcome!"

"Oh!" said Tom, surprised. The girls looked rather alarmed.

"What do you mean – something funny?" said Pippa.

"I don't know," said Andy. "But what we'll do is to see where that motor-boat is. It won't have seen our signal because it came in the night – and we know it's not anywhere this side of the island, or we would have seen it this morning. I vote we go to that rocky ledge where we get the best view of the second island and see if by any chance a boat has been able to get through the reef of rocks and sail into the quiet lagoon inside."

The four children made their way to the high rocky ledge.

Andy made them lie down flat and wriggle along as they reached it.

"Better not let ourselves be seen, if anyone *is* down there," he whispered. So, as flat as pancakes, they wormed their way to the rocky ledge – and when they got there, they had the biggest surprise of their lives!

In the quiet water that lay outside the second island was a large and powerful seaplane.

"Whew! Look at that!" whispered Andy. "I never thought of a seaplane! What an incredible thing!"

"Let's shout and wave," begged Pippa. "Then we can be rescued and go home."

"Haven't you seen the sign on the wings?" asked Tom, in a curious voice. The girls looked. Painted on each wing was a strange symbol.

"Who are they?" said Zoe, and she drew a deep breath. "Foreigners! Using these islands! Do they belong to them?"

"Of course not," said Andy. "But they're desolate, and out of the usual ships' course – and they're being used by these people as a base for something. They shouldn't be here."

"Well, what are we going to do?" asked Tom.

"We'll have to think," said Andy. "One thing is for certain. We won't show ourselves till we've found out a little more. We don't want to be captured."

"That's what that food was for, then – the people who come here," said Pippa. "I

suppose the seaplanes come over here for food and petrol. It's a good idea. How I wish we could get away and tell my father about it – he'd know what to do."

"Hadn't we better take down our signal while that seaplane is here?" asked Pippa. "If it happens to see it, those foreigners will know there are people on the island. And what about our boat? That might be seen too."

"I don't think so," said Andy. "It's well hidden between those rocks. But the signal had certainly better come down. We won't put it up any more. Come on, Tom, we'll take it down now."

"We'll come with you," said the girls. But Andy shook his head.

"No," he said. "From now on, somebody must keep a watch on that seaplane. We must find out all we can. We'll be back with you as soon as possible."

So the two girls were left behind while the boys ran across the island to take down their flapping signal.

"I don't know where in the world we would hide if we were discovered and hunted for," said Andy, rolling up the sail.

"There isn't a single place here to hide away in, not a cave or anything."

Tom felt rather uncomfortable. He didn't want to be hunted for on that bare island! "I wish we could see how many men there are in that seaplane," he said, "and what they're doing and everything."

"Where are your binoculars?" asked Andy suddenly. "They'd be just the thing to use. We could see everything as clearly as possible then!"

"And my camera, too!" said Tom, jumping for joy. "We could take some photographs of the seaplane, then everyone would have to believe us when we get back – if ever we *do* get back!"

"That's a great idea!" said Andy, really pleased. "If we could take some pictures of the seaplane with that sign showing up clearly, there wouldn't be the least doubt of our story when we got home. Tom, let's go and get your binoculars and your camera straight away."

They dumped the sail into a bush and ran to the shack. They took Tom's binoculars and checked the film on the camera.

"Better not use up all the film on that seaplane," said Andy. "There might be other interesting and extraordinary things to photograph, you never know!"

"Oh, I've got three or four films," said Tom. "I brought plenty with me. Come on, let's go back to the girls and see what they have to report."

The girls were very glad indeed to see the boys, and rushed to meet them. They had such a lot to tell.

"Andy! Tom! As soon as you had gone the men in the seaplane put out a funny little round sort of boat," said Pippa in excitement. "And they paddled to shore in it, and went to our cave. What a good thing the sea had washed away all our footprints!"

"It was, indeed," said Andy. "Tom, give me the binoculars. I want to have a look through them."

Andy stared through Tom's powerful binoculars. They seemed to bring the seaplane near enough to touch! He saw the little rubber boat left bobbing in the surf, while the men visited the cave – either to take something to it, or to bring something away, Andy did not know which.

"There seems to be someone in the seaplane," said Andy. "And look, there are some men coming from the cave!"

Andy could see them very clearly through the binoculars, and the others could see them too, though not so well, of course. To them the men looked like faraway dolls.

"They've gone to get food from the cave," said Andy in excitement. "And I bet there's a store of fuel somewhere else for them to get when they want to. Food, and fuel, just what I thought! Using these islands saves foreign planes from having to go hundreds of miles to their own country's stores. My word, we *have* stumbled on to something strange!"

The men jumped into their rubber boat and rowed back to the seaplane. Twice more they went to the cave and back. Then they climbed up into the plane and disappeared.

"I'm getting really hungry," said Tom at last. "Can't we go and get something to eat?"

"I'll stay here and keep watch, and you and the girls can go and get your lunch," said Andy. "Don't light a fire, whatever you do – someone will see the smoke. Use the stove if you want to cook anything. Bring me something to eat and drink later."

"Right," said Tom, and he and the girls wriggled off the high ledge. They stood upright as soon as they were out of sight of the seaplane and tore to their shack.

They ate a hurried meal, and did not cook anything at all. They made up a packed lunch for Andy and set off to take it to him. But halfway there they heard a noise. They stopped at once and listened.

"It's the seaplane taking off!" cried Tom – and then the sound came again, more loudly than ever.

"Look, there it is!" cried Pippa. "Drop flat to the ground or we'll be seen!"

CHAPTER TEN

AND NOW FOR THE THIRD ISLAND!

The seaplane roared over their island, rose higher and higher, and at last was nothing but a speck in the sky. The children were very glad that it had gone.

"It's a good thing our signal was taken down before it flew over the island," said Andy, eating the food that the others had brought him. "I couldn't warn you. It started up its engine all of a sudden, taxied over the smooth water there, and then rose into the air."

"Andy, do you think there's anything to be seen over on the other islands?" asked Tom.

"There may be," said Andy. "I think we ought to try and find out. That third island looks a peculiar shape to me – very long indeed, but very narrow. On the other side of it might be a good natural harbour for seaplanes. There may be heaps there."

"Well, we've only heard one so far," said Tom. "It doesn't seem as if they're very busy, if there are lots over there."

"No, you're right, Tom," said Andy. "Well, what about going to see what we can find? I don't quite know how we'll get to the third island – have to swim, I think."

"Shall we go tomorrow?" asked Tom eagerly. "We could cross to the second island at low tide in the morning and swim across to the third one."

"Yes, okay," said Andy. "But first we must find some sort of hiding place in case we're discovered."

"Well, there just isn't anywhere on this island," said Tom. "So we must hope no one will find us."

The children took turns at keeping watch on the second island from the rocky ledge. But nothing was to be seen at all. They went to bed early because the boys would have rather a hard and long day the next day. The girls were staying behind to keep watch.

"We'll have to clamber over that line of rocks first," said Andy. "And then we must cross the island and swim to the third one.

We shall have to be back on the second island in time to clamber over the rocks at the next low tide."

"I do wish we were going too," said Pippa. "Don't you think Zoe and I could climb over the rocks to the second island and wait for you there? It would be more fun for us to play about there than on this bare island. There are lots of bilberries there we could pick, they're lovely and sweet now."

"All right," said Andy. "But lie down flat under a bush or something if you hear a seaplane. You mustn't be seen."

"Okay," said Zoe.

So the next morning the four children once again climbed over the line of slippery rocks at low tide. They walked across the second island to where they could see the third island. It lay in the sea before them, like a long blue and brown snake. Beyond they could see one or two more islands.

"Do you really think you can swim so far, Tom?" asked Zoe doubtfully, as she looked at the wide spread of water.

"Of course," said Tom, who wasn't going to give up this adventure for anything. All the same, the distance was further than he had ever swum before.

The boys went down to the shore, waded into the water and began to swim. Andy was by far the stronger swimmer, but he kept close to Tom, just in case the younger boy got into difficulties. Tom began to pant a little, just over halfway across. Andy was fine still.

"Tread water a bit," he called to Tom. Tom did so, obviously unhappy.

"Try again, Tom," Andy went on. "It's no use going back! We're more than halfway across."

Tom tried again, but after about six strokes he could not swim any more. He turned on his back and floated.

Andy was really alarmed. "Tom, I'll have to help you."

"Thanks, Andy," said Tom, taking hold of Andy's shoulders, and Andy began to strike out valiantly with his brown legs.

It was very slow indeed. And now Andy began to get tired! Now what were they to do?

It wasn't long before neither Tom nor Andy had any strength left, and who knows

what would have happened if Andy had not felt something hard beneath his feet. It was a rock! They had come to a kind of rocky reef rather like the one they had climbed over from their own island to the second one, but this line of rocks was not uncovered by the tide.

"Tom! Tom! Put your feet down and feel where the rocks are!" gasped Andy. "We can stand there, and maybe feel our way along a bit till we come to the sandy bottom."

Tom soon found a foothold on the rocks under the water. He felt better at once. He and Andy made their way very cautiously over the sunken rocks, bruising their feet, but getting gradually nearer the shore. And at last they felt the rocks stop, and there was sand beneath their feet!

They lay on the sandy shore in the sun for a while, drying themselves.

"I feel fine now," Tom said, leaping to his feet. "Come on, Andy. Let's go up to the cliff-top and go across to the other side of this island."

The two boys climbed up the rough cliff and crossed the narrow width of the island to the cliff on the other side.

"Wriggle along on the ground now, just in case there's anyone about," said Andy. So both boys wriggled along on their fronts, and came at last to a place where they could see down to the water far below.

And what they saw there filled them with such astonishment and alarm that for at least five minutes neither boy could say a word!

CHAPTER ELEVEN

The Secret of the Islands

The sight that the two boys looked down upon was hardly to be believed. There was a very fine natural harbour of extremely deep water on the north-eastern side of the third island, and lying in this water were at least seven or eight submarines!

Submarines! A foreign submarine base in those deserted islands!

"It's a real nest of submarines," whispered Andy at last. "Foreign submarines! I can't believe it. My goodness, Tom, we've stumbled on an amazing secret!"

The boys stayed for some time looking down on the water. Some of the submarines lay like great grey crocodiles, humped out of the water. One or two were moving out of the harbour, their periscopes showing. It was a curiously silent place, considering that so many of these underwater ships were there. There was no noise of shouting, no noise of machinery, just a dull throbbing every now and again.

"They get fuel and food here," whispered Andy. "They are the small submarines – this harbour can easily take a dozen or more. It's a perfect place for them. Do you see how they haven't built any jetties or piers – not a thing that anyone could see, if any planes came over? All they would have to do then would be to sink under the water, and then there would be nothing to see. They store everything in the caves – it's amazing."

For a very long time the two boys lay watching the strange sight below. At first Tom had been so full of surprise and alarm, so swept with excitement, that he could think of nothing but the sight of the strange vessels. Then another thought came into his head and he turned to Andy.

"Andy," he said. "We've *got* to get home and tell what we've seen."

"I know," said Andy. "I'm thinking that too, Tom. And we are all in danger. If they knew we were spying on them like this I don't know what would happen to us."

"I don't care how much danger we're in,"

said Tom, and he didn't. "All I know is that we've *got* to go and tell people at home about this submarine base. But do you think anyone will believe us?"

"We'll get your camera and take a few photographs," said Andy. "Nobody can disbelieve photographs. And another thing we must do is get the boat off the rocks somehow and try to patch it up. It's our only way of getting back home."

They watched the harbour for a little while longer, and then wriggled along the top of the cliff till they came to some bushes. They went down by these and ran along till they came to the end of the harbour. Beyond lay a cove, and in it, drawn up on the sand, were a number of small boats. No one seemed to be about.

The sight of the little boats excited Andy. If only he could get hold of one! Then he and Tom could row round the third island, and get back to the second one safely. Andy knew perfectly well that Tom could not swim back, and he did not mean to leave the boy alone on this island with its submarines.

"Tom," he said, "see those boats? Well,

what about waiting till night-time, and then stealing one?"

"Good idea, Andy," said Tom, his face glowing with excitement. "But won't the girls be really worried if we don't swim back before low tide tonight?"

"We'll go to the cliff on the other side of this island and wave to them," said Andy.

"Okay," said Tom. "Let's go now."

The boys went to the other side of the island. After a while the girls appeared and waved to them. Pippa put the binoculars to her eyes.

"The boys seem really pleased and excited about something!" she said. "They're waving and pointing and nodding like anything. They seem to want us to understand something."

"Well, we'll know when they come back tonight," said Zoe philosophically.

The boys disappeared after a time and waited till the moon was behind the clouds, and gave only a pale light now and again. They slipped quietly down to the shore.

The boys stayed in the shadow of the cliffs for a few minutes, hearing no noise except the small sound of waves breaking on the sand. The boats were not far off, upturned in a row. No one was guarding them.

The boys crept over the silvery sand. "Take the boat on the left," whispered Andy. "It's just our size."

They came to the boat, and then they heard voices coming from the far side of the cliff. The boys could not hear any words, but the sound was enough to make them lie down flat beside the boat they had chosen.

Tom was trembling. Suppose they were found out just as they were taking the boat! It would be so unlucky. The boys listened until the sound of voices died away and then they cautiously lifted their heads.

"When the moon gets into that very thick cloud we'll turn the boat over and run her into the water," whispered Andy.

"Right," whispered back Tom. So when the moon slipped behind the dark clouds the boys did as planned. Then Tom got in and took the oars. Andy pushed the boat right out and leaped in himself.

Silently the boys rowed away from the shore, hoping that the moon would remain behind the cloud until they had pulled out of sight. No shout was heard. No running feet. They were undiscovered, so far!

Soon they were right round the narrow end of the third island. They rowed into the broad stretch of water between the second and third islands, then across to the shore below the cliff where they had left the girls.

Pippa and Zoe were watching there. They had been very worried when night had come and the boys had still not returned. And then Pippa, looking through the glasses when the moon had swum out into a clear piece of sky, had seen a little boat coming into the stretch of water between the two islands. She clutched Zoe's arm.

"Look! A boat! Who's in it?"

The girls looked and looked, their hearts beating loudly. The boat landed on the beach – and then the call of a seagull floated up the cliff.

"Andy!" cried Pippa, nearly falling down the cliff. "It's Andy! I'd know his seagull call anywhere!"

The boys climbed up the cliff and came to the rocky ledge. The girls fell on them and hugged them like bears, they were so relieved to see them again.

"The boat! Where did you get the boat?" whispered Pippa.

"What did you see? What did you find?" cried Zoe.

"We'll tell you all about it," said Andy, and the four of them sat close together on the cold, windy ledge, quite forgetful of the chilly breeze, talking and listening eagerly.

The girls could hardly believe the boys' story. It seemed quite impossible.

"And now that we've got a boat, we'll fill it full of food and water, and see if we can get home," said Andy. "It's the only thing we can do – and we must do it."

"But, Andy," said Pippa, "just suppose those people see their boat is missing – won't they search the islands?"

"Yes, they certainly will," said Andy. "So we'll have a good sleep tonight, take plenty of food from the cave, and see if we can make for home tomorrow."

"If only we can get away before they find that boat is missing!" said Tom. "Do you think we will?"

CHAPTER TWELVE

A Daring Adventure

The children did not have a very good night after they had rowed the stolen boat back to their own island. They slept rather late the next morning, for they had been too excited to sleep before midnight, and they were awakened by the throbbing noise that they had heard two nights before!

"The seaplane again!" said Andy, waking up at once and leaping to his feet. He ran to the open doorway of the hut and was just in time to see the plane soar overhead and land on the smooth water outside the second island.

"That means we can't get away today," said Tom at once. "We must get food into the boat, and we can't if that plane is there."

"No, we can't," said Andy. "But we might row over and try to take a few photographs of the submarine bay, Tom!"

"We'll have to be pretty careful."

"We will be," said Andy. "And now, what's for breakfast?"

There were more tinned sausages and baked beans in tomato sauce. They all ate in silence, thinking over everything that had happened.

"That seaplane may not stay long," said Andy. "It didn't last time. It will be busy that side of the island – so we'll row round the other side, where we won't be seen, go across to the third one, and tie up there."

They all got into the boat. The boys rowed to the furthest tip of the third island. Here there was a tiny beach with steep, overhanging cliffs – so overhanging that it almost seemed as if a big piece was about to fall off!

"Just the place," said Andy, pulling into the tiny beach. "Jump out, girls. Take the food with you. Give a hand with the boat, Tom. We'll run it up the beach and put it right under that dangerous piece of cliff. It'll be well hidden there."

They put the boat there and looked at it. The end of it jutted out and could be seen. Pippa ran to a seaweed-covered rock and pulled off handfuls of the weed.

"Let's make the boat into a rock!" she said, with a laugh. "Cover it with seaweed!"

"Good idea!" said Andy.

They all pulled at the seaweed, and soon the boat was nicely draped and looked so exactly like a seaweed-covered rock that no one could possibly guess it wasn't, even if they passed quite near it.

"That's good," said Andy. "Nobody will see it now."

Next, keeping close to tall bushes of gorse and bramble, the four children crept over the top of the island and came to the cliff below which was the boat-cove. Cautiously Andy parted some bramble sprays and peeped down to the beach below.

There were the rest of the little boats, still upturned. Nobody was about at all. As far as Andy could see, the stolen boat had not been missed. Good!

"Let's wriggle along to the next bit of the cliff," he said.

Going very slowly and cautiously, the four of them made their way to the top of the next cliff. They all lay on their tummies and peeped between the tall bracken. The girls drew a long breath of surprise.

"Where's your camera, Tom?" whispered Andy. Carefully Tom took it out of its waterproof case and set it for taking distant pictures.

"It's got the seaplane on the first two negatives," said the boy in a low tone. "I'll fill up the rest of the film with photos of the submarines. Then nobody can disbelieve us, or say we made it all up." He spent several minutes snapping away.

"We'd better get back," said Andy, when Tom had finished. "Then if we wait till the seaplane has left and go straight to the store-cave to fill our boat with food, we can start off tonight."

"All right," said Pippa, getting up. They hurried very cautiously back to the tiny beach where they had hidden their boat.

It was still there, beautifully draped with seaweed. Nobody had discovered it! The children dragged it down to the waves and jumped into it.

They took it in turns rowing. They were halfway round the second island, on the coast opposite to the one where the store-cave was, when a dreadful thing happened.

The seaplane chose that minute to leave

the water by the second island and to rise into the air ready to fly off!

The children had no time to rush their boat into shore and hide. They were out on the sea, clearly to be seen!

"Crouch down flat in the boat, so that the pilot may perhaps think there's nobody in it," ordered Andy. They shipped the oars quickly and crouched down. The seaplane rose up high, and the children hardly dared to breathe. They hoped so much that it would fly off without noticing them.

But it suddenly altered its course and began to circle round, coming down lower. It flew down low enough to examine the boat, and then, rising high, flew over the third island, and then flew down to the submarine bay.

Andy sat up, his face rather pale under its tan.

"That's done it," he said. "They saw us! Now they'll count their boats, find there's one missing – and come to look for us!"

CHAPTER THIRTEEN

Tom Disappears

The children looked at one another in great dismay. To think that the seaplane should have flown over just at that very moment! It was too bad.

"Well, we can't sit here looking at one another," said Andy, in a brave voice. "We've got to do something quickly. We'd better row straight round to the store-cave and fill the boat with food while we can," he went on. "Then we'll start out straight away and hope that the seaplane won't spot us out on the sea. It's the only thing to do."

It was a long row round to the cave, but they got there at last, quite tired out. There was nobody about. They beached the boat and jumped out. It was not long before they were in the Round Cave, carrying out stacks of tins and boxes to the boat.

"Look! We've got enough food to last for weeks!" said Tom.

"We may need it!" said Andy. "Goodness knows how far it is back home. I've not much idea of the right direction either, but I'll do my best."

Tom staggered out to the boat with heaps of things. Andy looked at the pile of food at the end of the boat and nodded his head.

"That's enough," he said. "We don't want to make the boat too heavy to row! Get in!"

They all got in. They rowed out beyond the reef of rocks where they had found a way in and then towards their own island. Andy wanted to get the rugs, for he was sure they would be bitterly cold at night.

"You girls jump out and go and fetch all the warm things you can find," said Andy. "And bring a cup or two and a knife. I've got a tin-opener."

The girls sped off to the shack in the hollow, and while they were gone the boys heard the sound they dreaded to hear, the noise of seaplane engines booming over the water!

"There it comes again!" said Andy angrily. "Always at the wrong moment. Lie down flat, Tom. I hope the girls will have the sense to do the same!"

The seaplane zoomed down low over the island, as if it were hunting for someone. Then it droned over the sea and flew round in great circles. Andy lifted his head and watched it.

"You know what it's doing?" he said. "It's flying round hunting the sea for our boat, just as a hawk flies over fields hunting for mice! It's a good thing we didn't set out straight away. I think now we'd better wait for the night to come, and then set out in the darkness. We should be seen as easily as anything if we try to go now."

They waited till the drone of the plane's engines was far away. It was hunting the waters everywhere for the stolen boat. Andy stood up and yelled to the girls, who were lying flat under a bush.

"It's gone for the moment. Help us to take out this stuff and hide it. If the boat is discovered here and taken away, and we're made prisoners on this island, we shall at least be sure of stores!"

"If we are able to start out tonight we can easily put back the food," said Tom. They all worked hard, and buried the tins and boxes under some loose sand at the top of the beach. They pulled the boat further up the beach and then sat down to rest, hot and tired.

And then poor Tom gave a squeal of dismay. The others jumped and looked at him in fright.

"Whatever's the matter?" asked Andy.

"My camera!" said Tom, his face a picture of horror. "My camera, with all those pictures I took! I left it in the store-cave."

"Left it in the store-cave!" said everyone. "Whatever for?"

"Well, I was afraid I'd bump it against the rocks, carrying it up and down those passages," said Tom. "So I took it off for a minute, meaning to put it on when we went. And I forgot."

"You idiot!" said Pippa.

"Don't call me that," said poor Tom, looking almost ready to cry.

"Well, idiot is too good a name," said Zoe. "Pinhead would be better. You can't possibly have got any brains if you do a thing like that, so you must be a pinhead with no brains at all."

Tom went very red. He blinked his eyes and swallowed a lump that had suddenly come into his throat. He knew how valuable the pictures were. How could he have forgotten his camera like that?

"Cheer up, Tom," said Andy. "I know what you feel like. I felt just like that when I found I'd forgotten to bring the anchor in the boat. It's awful."

Tom was grateful to Andy for not scolding him. But all the same he felt really dreadful. They had gone to such a lot of trouble to get those photographs, and now all because of his carelessness they had been left behind.

"I vote we have something to eat," said Andy, thinking that would cheer Tom up. But it didn't. For once in a while Tom had no appetite at all. He couldn't eat a thing. He sat nearby looking gloomily at the others.

The seaplane did not come back. The children sat and waited for evening to come, when they might start. Pippa yawned. "I must do something for the next two or three hours," she said, "or I shall fall asleep. I think I'll take the kettle and fill up the big water-barrel on the boat. That'll take several trips."

"Good idea," said Andy. "You and Zoe do that. I think I'll just wander up to the bush where we put the sail and see if it's still there. I don't think I've time to rig up some kind of a mast in this little boat so the sail won't be any good. But it might be useful to cover us with if it should happen to pour with rain."

The girls went off. Andy went across the island to the bush where he had put the sail.

Tom was left alone. "They don't want me with them," thought the boy, quite wrongly. "They think I'm stupid. *I* think I'm stupid too! Oh, dear, if only I could get my camera."

He thought of the reef of rocks that led to the second island. It wasn't a bit of use trying to climb over them because the tide was getting high now.

But then he thought of the boat! It really wasn't a great distance to row to the cave, from the beach where he was. How pleased the others would be, if he got back his camera!

The boy did not stop to think. He dragged the boat down the beach by himself, though he nearly pulled his arms out, doing it! He pushed it into the water and jumped in. He took the oars and began to row quickly round to the second island. He would land on the shore, then run quickly to the cave and get his camera.

"Then I'll be back here with it almost before the others know I'm gone!" he thought.

Nobody would have known what Tom

had done if Andy had not happened to look round as he went over the little island to find the old sail. To his enormous astonishment he saw their boat being rowed away!

The girls came back at that moment and shouted to Andy.

"What's the matter? Why do you look like that? Where's the boat?"

"Tom's gone off with it," said Andy, angrily.

"*Tom*! Whatever do you mean, Andy?" asked Pippa, in surprise.

"I suppose he felt upset about leaving his camera behind and he's gone to get it by himself," said Andy. "He really is an idiot. He may be seen and caught. I'm quite sure someone will be hunting for us soon."

The girls stared at Andy in dismay. They did not at all like the idea of their brother going off alone in the boat.

Andy could understand that Tom longed to get back his camera and put himself right with the others so that they no longer thought him careless and silly, but he did wish he hadn't gone off in their precious boat!

The three children waited and waited.

The sun sank lower. It disappeared over the skyline and the first stars glimmered in the darkening sky.

"Tom ought to be back by now," said Andy anxiously. "He's had plenty of time to get a dozen cameras! Whatever is he doing?"

Nobody knew. They sat there on the chilly beach, anxious and worried. If only, only Tom would come back! Nobody would scold him. Nobody would grumble at him. They just wanted him back again.

"I should think he's been caught," said Andy at last. "There can't be any other reason why he's not back. *Now* we're in a pretty fix! No Tom – and no boat!"

CHAPTER FOURTEEN

A Prisoner in the Cave

What had happened to Tom? A great many things. He had rowed safely to the beach where the caves lay hidden in the cliff behind. He had dragged the boat up the sand and had gone into the first cave.

He stumbled through the rocky archway and into the strange Round Cave, which was so full of food. He had no torch, so he had to feel around in the dark for his camera. It took him a long time to find it.

"Where *did* I put it?" wondered the boy anxiously. "Oh, if only I had a torch!"

But he hadn't. He felt over tins and boxes – and at last his hand fell on the box-like shape of his camera, safe in its waterproof covering!

"Good," Tom thought. "Now I'll just rush down to the boat and row back. I really must be quick or the others will be worried."

But Tom had a dreadful shock as he was about to make his way out of the Round Cave back to the beach. He heard voices!

The boy stood perfectly still, his heart beating fast. The voices came nearer. Was it the foreigners?

Alas for poor Tom – it *was*! Tom had not heard the boom of the seaplane coming down on the water. He had not seen a rubber dinghy putting off hurriedly to the cave. But now he could hear the voices of the men.

They had seen the boat on the beach, and had come to examine it. They soon saw that it was the stolen boat, which had now been missed and was being searched for.

Tom darted back into the Round Cave and hid behind a big pile of boxes. He felt quite certain he would be found, and as he crouched there, trembling and excited, he made up his mind very, *very* firmly that he would not say how many others had come to the islands with him. He would make the men think that he was the only one, then maybe the other three would not be hunted for.

"I've been such a fool to run into danger

like this," thought poor Tom. "But perhaps I can save the others from being hunted down."

The men came into the Round Cave. They had powerful torches which they flashed around, and almost at once they saw Tom's feet sticking out from behind a box.

They dragged him out and stood him up. They seemed most astonished to find that

he was only a boy. They had expected a man. They talked quickly among themselves in a language that Tom could not understand.

Then one man, who could speak English, said to Tom, "How did you get to this island?"

"I set off in a sailing boat and a storm blew up and wrecked me," said Tom. "You can see my boat off the coast of the next island, if you look."

"Is there anyone else with you on this island?" asked the man.

"There isn't anyone else here with me," Tom answered. "Search the cave, and see!"

The men did search the cave again, but found nobody, of course. They did not seem satisfied, however. Tom could see that they felt sure there were others to find.

"How did you find this cave?" asked the man who spoke English.

"By accident," said Tom.

"And I suppose you also found our boat by accident, and saw the submarines by accident?" said the man, in a very nasty voice. "Are you sure there is no one else here with you?"

"Quite sure," said Tom. "Wouldn't you see them in the cave, if there were?"

"We shall not take your word for it," said the man, with a horrid laugh. "We shall search this island and both those next to it, and if we find anyone else, you will be very, very sorry for yourself!"

"You won't find anyone!" said Tom, hoping that they wouldn't, and wishing he could warn Andy and the girls somehow. "Are you going to keep me prisoner?"

"We certainly are," said the man. "And as you seem so fond of this cave, we'll let you stay here! You've food to eat, and you won't be able to do any spying if you're here in this cave! We shall put a man on guard at the entrance, well hidden behind a rock, so if any friends of yours try to rescue you, they'll get a shock!"

Tom listened, his heart sinking into his shoes. What an idiot he had been! He was to be a prisoner, and if the others tried to find him they would be made prisoners too, for they would never guess a sentry was hidden behind the rocks, watching for them.

The men left a lamp in the cave for Tom. It was getting late and the boy was tired, but he could not sleep. He heard the men go out, and he knew a sentry had been placed by the rocks. He could not hope to escape. But he could try!

So, very quietly, he made his way through the rocky archway, down to the shore-cave below. But his feet set the stones moving here and there, and a voice came out of the darkness.

He could not understand what was said to him, but the voice was so stern that the boy fled back to the Round Cave at once.

He sat down again and wondered about the others. Would they guess he had gone to fetch his camera, and come to look for him when the tide uncovered the rocks the next day? If so, they would certainly be caught.

Andy and the girls sat up until they could keep awake no longer. They went back to the shack, curled up on their beds, and slept restlessly, worrying about Tom and the lost boat.

In the morning, Andy went out cautiously, wondering if the enemy had already landed a boat on their island to hunt for them. But he could see nothing unusual.

He sat talking to the girls as they prepared breakfast. "Tom has certainly been caught," he said. "There's no doubt about that, I'm afraid. Well, I know enough of Tom to know that he won't say *we* are here too. But they will certainly come and hunt for anyone else who might be here. We have to do two things – hide ourselves so that we can't possibly be found, and then think of some way of rescuing Tom."

"Oh dear! It all seems impossible," said Pippa, feeling very worried. Zoe began to cry.

"Don't cry, Zoe," said Andy, putting his arm round her. "We must all think hard and see what we can do to trick the enemy."

"But, Andy, how can we hide on this bare island?" said Zoe, drying her eyes and blinking away her tears. "They will beat all through the bracken and heather. There are no good trees to hide in. Not a single cave. Really, there isn't anywhere at all!"

"You're right, Zoe," said Andy. "It's going to be very difficult. But we must think of something. You see, if only we can hide and not be found we can somehow think of a way to rescue Tom – but if we are found we can't help Tom, and won't be able to escape and tell our secret!"

"It's a good thing we've got plenty of food hidden in the sand," said Pippa. "If we can manage to hide ourselves away we need not starve! We've only got to go and dig up that store of food!"

"Yes, that's very lucky," said Andy. "Hey, listen! That's the sound of a motor-boat, isn't it? They're coming! Quick! Where shall we hide?"

"We'd better rush over to the opposite side of the island," said Pippa, her face pale. "The first place they'll hunt is this side, where they land. Quick, Zoe!"

The three children slipped out of the shack and made their way up the rocky path. They were just out of sight when the motor-boat landed on the beach. They would be able to reach the other side of the island unseen but what could they do there? The shore there was nothing but rocks and sand – they would be found in two minutes!

CHAPTER FIFTEEN

THE ISLAND IS SEARCHED

Andy and the girls did not take long to reach the opposite shore of the island. It was sandy, but at one side was a mass of seaweed-covered rocks. It was impossible to hide behind them, for a moment's search would at once discover them.

Pippa stared and stared at the rocks nearby and then she gave such a squeal that Andy and Zoe jumped in fright.

"Shh!" said Andy angrily. "They'll hear you! Whatever's the matter?"

"I've thought of how to hide!" said Pippa breathlessly. "Can't we cover ourselves with sand, and then drape ourselves with seaweed, to look like rocks?"

"You know, that *is* an idea!" said Andy. "Quick! I'll cover you girls with sand at once. Come over here."

The three ran to the rocks. The tide was out, and the sand was hard but damp. Andy made the girls lie down together, and then he piled sand high over them, leaving a space over their noses for breathing. He only had his hands to do this, so it was hard work. Then he dragged great handfuls of seaweed from the rocks and threw it over the sandy mound. When he had finished, the girls looked exactly like the seaweed-covered rocks nearby! It was brilliant.

Andy covered with loose seaweed the untidy places he had made in the sand. Then he began to make a hole for himself, and to cover himself too. He draped himself with piles of seaweed and then poked up his head to look at the girls.

He really didn't know which of the rocks they were! He simply couldn't tell! He looked and looked, but not until one of the rocks moved a little did he see that it was the girls!

"Pippa! Zoe!" he called in a low voice. "As soon as you hear me screaming like a gull you must lie absolutely still. You look marvellous! I didn't know which rock you were till one of you moved."

They all lay quietly for a time and then Andy heard voices coming near. He cried like a seagull, and the girls then lay so still that not even the tiniest bit of seaweed above them moved at all.

The men slid down to the sandy shore, and looked round. One shouted something to the others and began to walk over to the rocks. Andy felt most alarmed.

The man came nearer. He stood near Andy and took out a packet of cigarettes. Andy heard him strike a match and knew that he had lit a cigarette.

The man threw the empty cigarette packet on to the sand, and puffed at his cigarette. A young gull, seeing the man throw the packet away, thought that it might be a piece of bread. It flew down to see, crying "Ee-oo, ee-oo, ee-oo!" very loudly.

Some other gulls flew down, and two stood on Andy and one stood on the girls! The children looked so exactly like rocks that the gulls really thought they were!

The men joined the one who was smoking a cigarette. They did not even bother to walk over the rocks. One man said it was plain there could be nobody hiding there for the gulls would not stand

about as they were doing if there was anyone hiding. They would know it and be suspicious.

For some time the men stood talking and smoking. Then they turned to go up the cliff again. One walked so near Andy that the boy could feel the thud of his footfall close by. Up the cliff climbed the men and disappeared over the top.

Andy cautiously lifted his head after a

while and looked around. There was no one to be seen.

"Zoe! Pippa!" he called, in a low voice. "I think the men are gone, but we must still be careful. Slowly and carefully take off the weed and shake yourselves free of the sand. Be ready to lie still at once if I say so."

But the men did not come back to the beach. The three children shook off the damp sand, threw the seaweed over the places where they had been lying and ran quickly to the shelter of the cliff, where none could see them, if they looked over.

"Phew!" said Andy, as they stood shivering under the cliff. "That was a narrow escape! One man very nearly trod on my hand under the sand!"

"I do feel cold," said Zoe, shivering and shaking. "It was horrid to be covered with the damp sand for so long."

She sneezed. Andy looked at her anxiously. It would never do for any of them to be ill just now. He made up his mind quickly.

"The men may be off the island now," he said. "I'll go and see. If they are we'll all tear across to the hut, light the stove inside and dry ourselves. We'll make some hot cocoa and get really warm."

The girls thought that was a great idea. Andy set off up the cliff. "Stay here till you hear my seagull cry," he said. "Then come as quickly as you can."

He made his way to the hollow where the old buildings were, and saw the motor-boat putting off from the shore! The men had given up the hunt and were going back to the third island. They had already searched the second one and had found nobody but Tom.

Andy tore back to the girls. He screeched like a gull. The girls at once climbed the cliff and ran across the island, feeling a little warmer as they ran. Andy lit the stove, which gave out a welcome heat.

"Take off your damp things and wrap yourself in the rugs," said Andy, who was already walking about with a rug draped over his shoulders. "I'm making some cocoa."

"Andy, what are you going to do now?" asked Pippa, feeling warmer at last. "We've got plenty of food, luckily, because we buried it all in the sand at the top of the beach out there, but we can't get away, because our boat's gone and we've lost Tom. Have we got to stay here for the rest of our lives?"

"Don't be silly, Pippa," said Andy. "Let's tackle one thing at a time, for goodness sake. The next thing is to rescue Tom! After that we'll think how to escape."

Pippa and Zoe cheered up. "I would like to rescue poor Tom," said Pippa. "He will be so lonely and upset. Where do you suppose he is?"

"In the cave where he left his camera, I expect," said Andy, pouring himself out another cup of cocoa. "And I'm pretty certain there'll be a guard somewhere at the entrance, for if there were not Tom would soon escape. So we'll see if there isn't some other way of rescuing Tom."

"But how can there be?" asked Pippa.

"I don't know yet," said Andy. "But I do know this – we thought it was impossible to hide safely on this bare little island, yet we did it! And so, though it sounds impossible to rescue Tom, there may be a way if we think hard enough. So now, let's all think hard!"

CHAPTER SIXTEEN

AN EXCITING DISCOVERY

Nobody could think how to rescue Tom. After all, if there was someone guarding the cave entrance, how could Andy possibly get in without being seen?

The boy gave it up after a time, and for a change he put on the only record that had not been broken in the storm. The girls listened, rather bored, for they had heard it scores of times.

"Turn it off, Andy," said Pippa. "If I hear that voice crooning that lullaby any more I shall go to sleep!"

Andy switched off the record player and went to the doorway of the shack. He was not afraid of the men coming back again for he was sure they thought there was no one on this island, at any rate.

A thought came into Andy's head. He went back to the girls.

"I think it would be a good thing if I

crossed to the second island tonight, when it's dark," he said. "I might be able to get in touch with Tom somehow and hear what has happened, even if I can't rescue him."

"Oh, Andy, we'll be left all alone," said Zoe in dismay.

"*We* don't mind that, if Andy can help Tom," said Pippa. "We'll stay here in the hut, Andy, and try to sleep while you go. But do be careful, won't you?"

"I'll be careful," said Andy. "I don't want to be taken captive, too."

So that night, when he had only the starlight to guide him, for the moon was not up, Andy crossed the line of rocks to the second island. He went very cautiously, for he did not want a single sound to come to the ears of anyone on the cave-beach.

He waded through the shallow water to the sand at the nearer end of the beach. He stood there, listening, and not very far off, close against the cliff where the cave-entrance was, he heard a cough!

"That's it!" said Andy to himself. "Thanks for that cough, dear sentry! I now know exactly where you are. You are behind the big rock at the cave opening.

Well, I shall not go near you!"

The boy stood quite still for a while, listening. The sentry most obligingly cleared his throat again very loudly. Andy grinned. He made his way carefully round the end of the cliff and then began to climb up, feeling his way cautiously. The cliff there was not very steep, and Andy was soon at the top. He had not made a single sound.

He found a little hollow where heather and gorse grew thickly. He crept under an overhanging piece of bush, piled the heather beneath him, and slept peacefully. He knew he could do nothing till morning came, and he could see where he was.

The sun rose and Andy awoke. He was stiff and he stretched himself and yawned. He was hungry, but there was nothing for him to eat but bilberries.

He wriggled carefully to the edge of the cliff and looked over. Almost below him was the sentry he had heard the previous night, behind a rock at the cave entrance. As Andy looked down he saw a boat coming to the shore, and a man stepped off and walked up the beach to change places with the sentry. They stood talking for a while and then the first sentry went to the boat, yawning, and the new one settled down to his task of waiting and watching.

Andy sat and thought. He wriggled back to a place where he imagined he must be exactly over the Round Cave. He wondered if Tom could hear him, if he drummed on the ground with his feet. After all, the boy could not be very far below, for the Round Cave was fairly high up in the cliff.

And then a most extraordinary thing happened, so startling that Andy's heart jumped almost out of his body!

A groan came from somewhere under his legs! Andy was lying on the heather, and when the groan came, he shot his legs up beneath him and stared at the place where the groan had come from as if he simply couldn't believe his ears!

A smaller groan sounded, more like a long yawn. Andy stared. Heather couldn't yawn or groan! Then what was it?

Very cautiously and gently, the boy turned himself about and began to feel in the heather. He pulled it to one side, and to his enormous astonishment he found a hole below the roots of the heather – a hole that must lead down to the Round Cave.

Andy felt so excited that he began to tremble. "No wonder that cave didn't smell as musty and stuffy as we expected it to," he thought. "There's an airhole leading right down to it! Wow! I wonder if there's any chance of rescuing Tom this way."

He pulled up the heather and examined the hole. The earth was dry and sandy. Andy scraped away hard, and found that it

was quite easy to make it bigger. Just suppose he could make it big enough to get down, or for Tom to get up!

"I knew there'd be a way if we didn't give up hope!" thought the excited boy. "I just knew it!"

He crawled to the top of the cliff and looked over it. The sentry was there still, and he was busy eating his breakfast. He was quite safe for some time.

Andy crawled back to the hole. He scraped about a little more, and then lay down with his face in the hole. It seemed to go down and down into the darkness.

Andy spoke in a low voice. "Tom! Are you there?"

And was Tom there? Yes, he was! He had been in the Round Cave, alone and lonely, ever since he had been caught. It had seemed ages to him. The boy had worried dreadfully about the others. He had eaten a little of the food around him, but he had no appetite now. He was miserable and frightened, though he would not show this to any of the sentries who occasionally came up the rocky passage to see if he was all right.

The man who could speak English had come to see him the evening before.

"We have searched the first island and this one," he had told Tom. "We have found your shack, and we have found your friends, too!"

Tom's heart sank when he heard this, but he said nothing. He did not know that the man was really telling lies, hoping to trap Tom into saying something that would show him there were others to be found.

"I tell you we have found your friends," said the man. "They fought hard but they have been captured."

Tom stared at the man in surprise. He knew quite well that the girls would not fight men. What did this man mean? Could he be telling a lie?

Then Tom suddenly knew that the man was hoping to trap him into saying something about the others. This man did not know that the "others" were only two girls and a boy. He did not even know for certain that there were any others!

"Well, two can play at a game of pretend like that!" thought the boy. So he put on a face of great surprise and said:

"What! There *are* others on these islands then? I wish I'd known, I could have asked them for help!"

The man looked surprised. So perhaps this boy had no friends then? Could it be that he was really alone? The man did not know what to think. He said no more but turned and went out of the cave. Tom couldn't help feeling pleased. The man had thought he might trap him, but he felt sure *he* had tricked the man!

It was very lonely in the Round Cave. Tom slept heavily all the night through, but found the day very, very dull.

He sat on a box and groaned deeply. Then he yawned loudly. He was bored. He was lonely.

He sat there, doing nothing; and then he heard a very peculiar noise above his head – a kind of scraping noise. Tom wondered what it could be.

The scraping noise went on, and then something happened that made Tom leap up in fright.

A strange hollow voice came into the cave from somewhere! It ran all round the cave and Tom could just make out the words. The funny deep voice said, "Tom! Are you there?"

It was really Andy's voice, of course, coming down the hole to the cave, and the hole had made it sound deep and strange, not a bit like Andy's.

Tom trembled and said nothing. He couldn't understand this strange voice suddenly coming into the cave. So Andy spoke again.

"Tom! It's Andy! Are you there?"

The voice rumbled round the cave, but this time Tom was not so scared. He answered as loudly as he dared.

"I'm here! In the Round Cave!"

Tom's voice came up to Andy, all muddled and jumbled, for Tom was not near the opening of the hole. Andy could not make out what he said, but he knew it was Tom speaking.

"Good!" he thought. "Tom's in there all right. I'll speak to him again and see if I can find out what's happened to him."

So once more Andy's voice came rumbling down into the cave. "Tom! I'm speaking down a hole that must somehow lead into your cave. See if you can find it and speak up it. I can't hear you properly. But whatever you do, don't let anyone hear you speaking to me."

Tom felt excited. Good old Andy! He got up and began to hunt around for the hole that led upwards to Andy. He must find it, he just had to!

CHAPTER SEVENTEEN

A Brilliant Escape

Tom picked up the lamp and hunted around the cave. As he was doing this he heard the steps of the sentry coming up the rocky passage to the Round Cave. At once Tom sat down and began to sing loudly the lullaby that was on the unbroken record.

Hush, hush, hush,
You mustn't say a word.
It's time for hush-a-bye,
My little sleepy bird.

These were the words of the rather silly lullaby song on the record. But they did very well indeed for a warning to Andy not to say anything for a moment! The sentry heard the boy singing, peeped in at him, said something that Tom didn't understand, and went out again. Tom went on singing the lullaby for a long time till he felt quite sure the sentry was not coming back.

Then he stopped singing and hurriedly began to hunt for the hole again. It didn't seem to be anywhere! The roof of the cave was not very high, and by standing on boxes and tins Tom could examine nearly every inch of it. But he could not find a hole that led upwards.

Andy's voice came booming down again: "Tom! Have you found the hole?"

The voice was so close to Tom's ear that the boy nearly fell off the box he was standing on. He held up the lamp to the place where the voice came from. It was at the point where roof and wall met, at the back. The roof was of rock, but the wall just there was only of sand. Tom put his hand up and felt a cold draught blowing down the hole.

"Andy! I've found the hole!" he said, putting his head to it. "But it's too small to get up it unless I could make it larger. What's it like at your end?"

"I can easily make it as large as I like by scraping at it," said Andy. "Can you make your end large, too, do you think?"

Tom scraped at it with his hands. He

could easily scrape the wall away, but not the roof. "I might perhaps be able to," he said. "But I'd want something to do it with – I've nothing but my hands."

"I've nothing but my hands either," said Andy, "and they're bleeding already from scraping at the soil. Listen, Tom, I'll go back to the girls soon, when the rocks are uncovered, but I can't wait till night. So I want you to call to the sentry and pretend that you want his help in undoing a tin of food or something. Okay? Then while he is in the cave with you, I'll creep over the rocks safely without being seen, and get back."

"All right," said Tom. "What will you do then?"

"I'll collect something for us to work at the soil with," said Andy. "And I'll bring it back tonight. Then maybe we can make the hole large enough for you to crawl up. I don't think it's more than about two metres long. Now, wait to hear my seagull call, Tom, then yell for the sentry, and I'll make a dash for the rocks as soon as I see him go into the cave."

Everything worked well. When Tom

heard Andy's seagull cry he shouted for the sentry, and the man went into the cave to see what was the matter.

He found that Tom had got a large tin of ham, and seemed to have lost the tin-opener. The sentry hadn't one either, and he spent a very long time trying to open the tin with his pocket-knife. He ended up cutting his thumb very badly, and Tom produced a handkerchief and spent a long time binding the man's thumb, glad to keep him in the cave so long.

Andy had plenty of time to escape back over the rocks. He knew them well now, and leaped from rock to rock easily. He was back in the shack in no time, it seemed!

The girls were thrilled to see him and he had to sit and tell them all he had done. When they heard about the hole leading down to the Round Cave the girls were tremendously excited.

"So you see," finished Andy, "I plan to get Tom out that way tonight, and I must take back with me something to dig and scrape with."

"Here's an old bit of wood with some pretty big nails in it at one end, all sticking out," said Pippa. "Would that do?"

"Yes, that's fine," said Andy. "Is there a bit for Tom?"

They found an old bit that would do. And then Andy said such a funny thing.

"I'll take the record player too! And the one record!"

The girls stared at him. "The record player!" said Pippa at last. "Whatever for? Are you mad?"

"It does sound rather mad, I know," said Andy. "But I want it for something. I'll tell you afterwards. It won't sound quite so mad then!"

Andy had a very good meal, for he was awfully hungry. Then he settled down to sleep, for, as he said, he would not have much of a night *that* night!

After midnight, the boy went over the rocks again, carrying the pieces of rough wood with nails in, and the record player slung carefully over his shoulder. He reached the shore safely and made his way cautiously up the cliff.

And very soon Tom, half asleep, heard the strange hollow voice rumbling round his cave once more. "Tom! Are you asleep!"

Tom climbed on the chest and put his head to the hole. "Hi, Andy!" he said. "I'm not asleep. I've been waiting and waiting for you!"

"There's a bit of wood with nails in coming down the hole," said Andy. "Scrape at your end with it and try your best to make the hole larger. I've got one too. I'll scrape my end. Mind that you don't get your eyes full of bits falling down."

The two boys set to work. Both of them scraped and dug for all they were worth. The soil was very dry and sandy, and was easy to move. Heaps of it fell down to Tom's end and he had to dodge it every now and again.

At last Andy's hole was quite big enough to get into. He called softly to Tom, "How are you getting on? I've got a rope I can let down to you if you're ready."

"I'm nearly ready," answered Tom, scraping hard. "Just a minute or two more!"

And then, at last, his end was large enough to climb into! The boy put another chest on the top of the one he was standing on and knelt upon it. His head and shoulders were right in the hole – he stood up and almost disappeared in the long, narrow funnel.

"Wait a minute, Tom," said Andy. "I've got something I want to let down on the rope. It's the record player."

"The what?" asked Tom in astonishment, thinking he couldn't have heard correctly.

"The record player," said Andy. "I'm afraid, Tom, you may make rather a noise climbing down the cliff, and the sentry might think you had escaped – but if I set the record going, singing that silly lullaby you sang yesterday, he will think it's you still in the cave and he won't come and see what the matter is. So I'm going to let it down, and you must set it right, and tie a bit of string to it so that I can pull the switch and set the record going when I think it's best to."

"Well!" said Tom. "You think of everything!" The record player came bumping down the hole, on the end of the rope. Tom put it carefully behind a big chest and set the needle ready on the outside edge of the record. He tied a long piece of string to the starting-switch, and then tied the other end to the rope that Andy had let down with the record player.

"Pull it up, Andy," he said. "But carefully, please, because the string's on one rope and we don't want to break the needle by jerking the string too hard!"

Andy drew up the rope, untied the string on the end of it, and tied it to a heavy stone for safety. Then he called to Tom. "That's done. You come up now, Tom. Here's the rope. Tie it round your waist and I'll help you up the hole by pulling – and remember, *don't* forget your camera!"

Tom stood on the highest chest and began to scramble up the hole. There were plenty of rough ledges each side where he could put his feet. Andy hauled strongly on the rope, and Tom's head suddenly appeared through the hole by Andy's feet!

"Good!" said Andy. "Climb out!"

Tom climbed out. He sniffed the fresh breeze with delight, for it had been pretty stuffy down in the cave. Andy undid the rope from round Tom's waist. "Now you must get down the cliff as best you can without noise," he said. "Wait for me at the edge of the rocks, won't you? I'll give you a

hand over those because I know them better than you do now."

Tom went to the cliff and began to climb down. Halfway down he slipped, and kicked out quickly to prevent himself from falling. A whole shower of stones fell down the cliff. The sentry, half-dozing, shouted at once.

Andy knew it was time to pull the string that was tied to the record player! He jerked it. The switch slid to one side and the record began to go round. The needle ran over the record and the lullaby began to sound in the cave.

The sentry heard it and thought it was Tom singing. He felt satisfied that his prisoner was still in the cave, as the song went on, and settled himself down again in a comfortable position.

Andy slipped down the cliff to where Tom was waiting for him by the line of rocks.

"Didn't I make a row?" Tom whispered. "But I couldn't help it."

"It's all right! I set the record going and the sentry thinks you're busy in the cave, singing yourself to sleep," said Andy with a low chuckle. "Come on, we've no time to lose!"

CHAPTER EIGHTEEN

HEAVE-HO! HEAVE-HO!

Over the line of rocks the boys slipped and climbed, Tom following Andy closely.

They made their way to the shack, which was in darkness, for Andy had forbidden the girls to show a light of any sort in case the enemy saw it. Zoe and Pippa were lying together on their heather bed in the darkness, fast asleep.

Zoe heard the boys come in and she sat upright in bed at once. "Is that you, Andy?"

"Yes, and Tom too!" said Andy. Pippa awoke then, and the four of them sat on one bed, and talked.

"I was such an idiot to try and get my camera back," said Tom. "I never thought of being caught. And now the boat is gone."

"There's only one thing we can do," said Andy. "And that's to get our boat off the rocks early tomorrow morning somehow, and refloat her. I've noticed she seems to have moved a bit, and it may be that the tides have loosened her. Perhaps the two rocks that held her are not holding her quite so fast now. Anyway, it's our only chance."

"Yes, we'll try and do that," said Pippa. "Tom's escape is sure to be discovered sometime tomorrow, and this time such a search will be made that I know we'll all be found."

"Well, let's sleep for an hour or two till dawn," said Andy. "We can't do anything at the moment."

So they lay down on their beds and slept until Andy awakened them two hours later.

The children slipped across the island and came to the beach where they had first landed. The tide was not very high yet, and it was possible to reach the boat without too much difficulty.

It was not long before all the children had reached their boat, and were clambering up the wet and slippery deck.

The boys went down into the little cabin. It had water lying at the bottom. Andy ripped up the planks and examined the boat underneath the floor of the cabin.

Then he came out and let himself down the side of the boat, disappearing under the water to feel the bottom of the boat. The girls and Tom watched him anxiously.

When Andy joined them on the slanting deck he looked very cheerful.

"Do you know, there's not much wrong!" he said. "I reckon I could patch her up fairly quickly."

Tom and Andy went back over the rocks to fetch a rope. Andy felt sure that if they all tugged at the boat at high tide, they could get her off the rocks and float her to the beach, where it would not be difficult to patch her up.

"If only we can do it all before those men come again," said Tom. "I wonder if they've discovered that I've gone?"

"Don't let's think about that," said Andy.

The boys found all the rope they had and wound it firmly round their waists. They went back to the boat and fastened strong double strands of rope to the bows. Then, holding firmly to the rope, they clambered over the rocks back to the sandy beach, wet through. The tide came up higher and higher and the children had to stand up to their waists in the water, for the rope would not reach right to the shore.

"Look! There's an enormous wave coming!" shouted Andy. "Pull on the rope, all of you, as soon as the wave strikes the ship! *Heave*!"

They all pulled, and every child felt the ship give a little as the wave lifted her and the rope pulled her.

"There's a monster coming!" shouted Tom. "Look at it! It'll sweep us off our feet!"

The wave struck the boat and the rope dragged at her at the same moment. She shivered and groaned as she tried to escape from the rocks that held her. She slipped a little way forward.

The giant wave struck the children next, and all of them went down under it, even Andy. None of them let go of the rope. They all held on for dear life, so it was not long before they were standing up again, gasping and spluttering, salt water in their mouths and noses, but all of them determined to heave again as soon as the next big wave came.

"Look how the boat has moved!" yelled

Andy, in great delight. "She's almost off the rocks!"

The boat had moved a good deal. Andy waited patiently for the next big wave to come – and sure enough, it was a monster!

The children gave a yell.

"Look at that one!"

"It'll knock us all over again," said Zoe, afraid. But she didn't let the rope go.

The wave grew bigger and higher as it came nearer to the rocks on which the boat lay. It began to curl over a little, and then it struck the rocks, and the boat too.

"HEAVE!" yelled Andy, in a voice as enormous as the wave! And they all heaved.

The great wave blotted the boat from their sight and came raging towards them. Pippa gave a shout of fear.

"Hold on!" shouted Andy, half afraid himself. The wave swept them all off their feet, and alas, swept them all from the rope too, except Andy, who held on with all his might.

The other three children were taken like corks, rolled over and over, and flung roughly on the sand at the edge of the sea. Then the great wave ran back down the beach, gurgling and foaming.

Pippa sat up, crying. Zoe lay still, quite stunned for the moment. Tom sat up, furiously angry with the wave!

As for Andy, he was under water, still clinging to the rope, but as soon as he struggled to his feet he gave a gurgling shout and tried to clear his throat of the salt water there.

"The boat! Look! She's off and floating!"

They all looked – and there was the little fishing-boat, safely off the rocks, bobbing about on the sea that swirled high over the other rocks.

"Come in and help me, quick, before any other big waves come!" yelled Andy. "We can get her into shore now. Quick, Tom!"

The three battered children, dripping wet, ran bravely into the sea again. They caught hold of the rope and pulled hard.

And the boat came bobbing into the shore! The children dragged the rope up the beach and the boat followed, scraping its bottom at last on the sand.

"We've got her!" shouted Andy, doing a kind of dance on his tired legs. "We've got her! Now we'll just see what we can do!"

CHAPTER NINETEEN

A Shock for the Children

The four children were so excited at getting their boat off the rocks that at first they could do nothing but laugh and chatter and clap their hands.

The boat lay on her side in the shallow water. Andy examined her carefully. He was sure that if he could nail planks inside, just where she had been smashed by the rocks, he could patch her up well enough for her to sail home.

"She'll let water in, but we can bail her out all the time," said Andy. "I'll patch her up enough just to get her sailing safely."

Tom fetched the tools from the shack and the box of nails and screws and bolts. Andy meant to be very busy indeed. Somehow or other that boat had to be finished before Tom's escape was known.

After a hurried breakfast, they all set to work under Andy's orders. Andy stripped some of the wood from the roof of the cabin for patching.

The sound of the hammer echoed over the island. "Do you think they'll hear?" asked Pippa anxiously.

"Can't help it if they do," said Andy. "We can't hammer without noise! Pass me the biggest nails you've got, Tom."

They all worked steadily for the whole of the morning. And at last Andy heaved a sigh of relief.

"Well, I think that'll do. She won't last long without being bailed out, because I can't patch her really properly, but Pippa and Zoe can easily bail out while you and I sail the boat, Tom."

"Is she ready?" ask Zoe eagerly.

"As ready as I can make her," said Andy. "Now, you two must go and get all the rugs, and Tom and I will get the food from where we buried it under the sand, at the top of our own beach by the shack. We'll pile in everything we can, push her out into the water and sail off!"

The four of them set off to fetch everything. They felt cheerful and excited. It might take them ages to get home, but at last they were going to leave these strange unknown islands safely, and take their secret with them!

The girls gathered up the rugs. The boys tied the tins and boxes together and staggered over the island with their heavy load, back to the boat again.

It was difficult climbing down the cliff so heavily laden, but they managed it safely. The girls threw down the rugs on the deck, and the boys packed the food into the cabin. Now they could go!

They all took hold of the rope to drag it down to the sea, but even as they took hold of it, what a shock they had! A loud voice shouted to them from round the corner of the cliff.

"Stop! Halt!"

The children stopped hauling the boat and stared round. They saw the foreigners – four of them! One of them was the man who spoke English, and it was he who was shouting.

The children stared in fright at the four men, who came quickly over the beach.

"So! There are four of you – and all children! This is the boy who escaped – ah,

you thought you were very clever, didn't you?"

"I did, rather," said Tom boldly. He felt frightened, but he wasn't going to show it!

"You took your boat off the rocks, and thought you would escape safely, didn't you?" said the man mockingly. "Well, you made a mistake. We shall now take the boat away, and you shall remain prisoners on this island for as long as we want you to! Take the food and blankets out again. You will need those if you live here for months!"

The children sulkily took out all the food and rugs they had so cheerfully put into the boat.

"Now we are going," said the man who spoke English. He gave a rapid order to the other men, who ran off round the cliff and then reappeared in a small boat, bobbing on the waves. It was plain that they had landed round the cliff, watched the children, and then come to catch them.

Andy and the others had to watch the men drag their boat down to the sea and launch it. They had tied their little rowing boat behind it, and now, waving mockingly to the children, they made their way over the water, round the cliff, and out of sight, rowing Andy's boat along swiftly.

Wearily the children gathered up the old rugs and all the food and made their way up the cliff, across the island and back to their shack. They packed the food on the floor in a corner and threw the rugs on the beds.

"Andy, what are you thinking about?" asked Tom. "You look so stern. You're not angry with *us*, are you?"

"No," said Andy. "We all did our best, and we've got to do our best again. I tell you, Tom, we've *got* to leave this island! Somehow, we've got to get away and tell our secret. As long as those men remain hidden in these islands, able to come here whenever they need food or fuel, then people must be in danger."

"But how *can* we get away now our boat's gone?"

"I'll think of a way," said Andy. "I'm going off by myself now, to puzzle a way out of this fix."

The boy slipped out of the shack. He climbed the cliff and sat in the heather, his blue eyes fixed on the skyline. For two hours he sat there, puzzling and worried, and then he straightened himself and got up. He went down to the others, his eyes shining and his head up.

"I've thought of a way," he said proudly. "I've thought of a way at last!"

CHAPTER TWENTY

Andy Makes a Plan

Tom, Zoe and Pippa looked at Andy, excited.

"Have you really thought of a way, Andy?" asked Pippa. "You are clever."

"Well, it's no use us trying to take one of their boats again, or to get our own boat back," said Andy. "And it's no use putting up a signal to passing ships, for two reasons – one is that I am perfectly certain no ship ever passes near these islands, or they would have discovered the secret of the submarines before this – and the second reason is that I am pretty sure we wouldn't be allowed to have a signal up anyhow!"

"Go on," said Tom, feeling sure Andy had got a very good idea coming.

"Well, my idea is this – we'd better make a raft!" said Andy. "We can't get a boat or make one, but we could make a rough kind of raft, and get a mast of some sort to rig a sail on. We've plenty of food to take with us, and you and I, Tom, could set off on it to try and make for home. I daren't take the girls – they would be so cold on an open raft, and they would be safer here."

"Not take us!" cried Pippa indignantly. "Of course you'll take us! We won't be left behind, will we, Zoe?"

"Listen, Pippa, you're only ten years old and not very big," said Andy patiently. "If we take you it will make things much more difficult for Tom and for me. If we get home safely we can have you rescued at once. If we don't get home you will at least be safe on the island."

The girls thought it was very unfair. They couldn't know that Andy didn't feel at all certain of ever getting home, and was very much afraid of the girls being washed overboard when big waves came.

Andy was quite firm about it, and the girls eventually listened to his plans. Tom wondered what the raft was to be made of.

"We shall have to pull our wooden hut to pieces and use the planks," said Andy. "Luckily we've got plenty of nails to use."

"But what shall we live in if we pull

down the shack?" asked Pippa in dismay.

"I've thought of that," said Andy. "You see, if we start pulling down the shack the enemy are bound to notice it and will guess what we are doing. Well, I thought we could make it look as if our hut had fallen down on us, and I could ask the men to give us a tent to live in instead. Then we could live in that, and quietly make our raft from the fallen-down shack!"

"That really *is* a good idea," said Tom. "We get the two things we want – somewhere else to live and wood to make a raft – and the foreigners actually help us without knowing it!"

"Yes," said Andy, grinning round at the other three. "We'd better wait a day or two, though, because we're bound to be watched a bit at first, to see if we've any other ideas of escape. We won't do anything suspicious at all for the next few days."

"All right," said the others, and so for the next few days the children just played about, bathing, fishing, paddling, and the foreigners, who sent a man over every day at noon, saw nothing to make him think that the children had any plans at all.

"I think there's going to be a storm," said Andy, on the third evening. "That would be a good reason for our shack to fall down, I think! As soon as that man has come and gone today we'll turn the shack into a ruin!"

The man came, looked round the island and went. As soon as he had gone the children set about the hut. Andy removed nails and took out planks. He hammered part of the roof away and made a big hole. He made one side of the hut so weak that it fell in on top of the girls' bed.

"Doesn't it look a ruin now!" said Pippa, with a giggle. "We'd better spread the sail over that side of the hut, Andy, or the rain will come in tonight."

"Okay," said Andy.

"And tomorrow we'll pretend that in the storm our hut was blown in – and we'll bandage up Pippa's head as if the hut fell on top of her, and bandage my leg too. And we'll beg pathetically for a tent!"

Just then there was a loud clap of thunder and the storm began properly. It was not a very bad one, but the wind blew fiercely, and Andy and Tom had to weight the old sail down to prevent it from being swept away.

In the morning the children took the sail and hid it safely. They made the shack look as if the wind had almost blown it down.

“Now I’ll tie up Pippa’s head in my big handkerchief,” said Andy, taking out a rather dirty hanky. “And I’ll use a rag to tie my leg up with. We’ll pretend we got hurt in the night.”

When the man came to look at the children and go over the island as usual, he was surprised to find Pippa bandaged up, and Andy limping.

Andy hailed him. "Hi! Our shack has fallen down! Come and see!"

The man went to look. He could not speak English, but he understood at once that the shack had fallen down on the children during the storm. Pippa sat on the ground, pretending to cry, holding her head in her hand. Zoe was trying to comfort her.

"We want a tent to sleep in," said Andy. The man did not understand. Tom took out his notebook and drew a tent in it. Then the man understood. He nodded his head, walked away and set off in his boat.

"I hope he comes back with a tent," said Tom. "You'd better go up the cliff, Pippa, so that if the man comes back he won't ask to see your head."

Pippa and Zoe went off. Tom and Andy waited for the man to return. He came back in about three hours – and he'd brought a tent! The man put the tent down on the beach, showed Andy the ropes and pegs with it and went off again in his boat.

"Good!" said Andy. "We'll put this tent up in a sheltered place in the next cove. We don't want the man visiting this hollow too often, or he may notice that the shack is gradually disappearing!"

The man came again the next day and Andy showed him where they'd put the tent. Andy limped about with the rag still on his leg, which made the others want to smile, but the man did not once guess that it was all pretence.

The weather was not so good now. The sun was not warm, and clouds sailed over the sky, bringing showers of rain at times. The children often had to sit in the tent, and they longed to begin making the raft.

"I don't want to start it till I'm sure the man has forgotten about the tumbledown shack," said Andy. "Yesterday he brought his boat in to this beach instead of the next one, and hardly looked over the island at all. If he comes to this cove today, we can begin the raft this afternoon."

The man came at noon as usual. This time he brought a large supply of food, and pointed to three fingers and shook his head.

"I think he means he won't be back for three days," said Andy. He nodded to the man who, instead of looking over the island as he usually did, got straight back into his boat and rowed off.

"Well, if that isn't a bit of luck!" said Andy joyfully, as soon as he had gone. "He's brought us a fantastic supply of food that will just do brilliantly for the raft! We can safely begin building it this afternoon!"

CHAPTER TWENTY-ONE

The Building of the Raft

The four children tackled the shack that afternoon and tore out as many planks as they could, and by the end of the day they had sixteen planks of different sizes piled up. Andy was pleased.

"If we can get as many as that tomorrow, we'll be able to make a really fine raft," he said. "Tom, you *are* saving all those long screws and nails, aren't you? We shall need them soon."

"Yes, they're all safe," said Tom.

"Do you think we'd better hide these planks in case the man *does* come tomorrow, although we feel sure he won't?" asked Pippa.

"Well, perhaps we had better," said Andy. So he and Tom took the planks one by one and hid them in thick heather. Then they went to have a good meal, which the girls had been getting ready. There was cold ham, baked potatoes, and tinned asparagus tips which the man had brought yesterday.

To follow they had sliced pears with condensed milk, and hot cocoa. Then they fell into bed.

They were all tired, and they fell asleep on their heathery beds almost as soon as they had cleared up, and did not wake till late the next day. Andy could not make up his mind whether to get on with the raft or not.

"I'm pretty sure that fellow meant he wouldn't come for a few days," Andy said. "But if he did happen to come and found us at work on a raft, it would be too disappointing for anything."

"Well, one of us could go up to the rocky ledge and keep watch all the time, couldn't we?" said Pippa eagerly. "We could easily see anyone coming, and give warning in time to let you and Tom hide everything."

"That's a good idea," said Andy. "Take it in turns of about two hours each. You go first, Pippa, and Zoe next."

So Pippa went up to the rocky ledge and sat there. No boat was to be seen, but seaplanes flew over many times during the day, their engines roaring loudly. Three came down in the calm water opposite the cave-beach. Pippa watched them carefully.

"Well, there's one thing that's lucky," said Andy with a grin. "Those seaplanes make such a noise that no one could possibly hear the sound of any hammering today, so I vote we get on with it and make as much noise as we like now there's a chance!"

So Andy and Tom nailed twelve big planks crosswise to twelve others below. Then on top of the two crosswise rows Andy nailed yet another row of shorter planks to make the raft really solid and heavy.

The boys added a kind of rim to the raft to prevent things rolling off too easily. It was a very solid-looking affair that began to take shape by the time that night came.

Andy had found a strong post that would do for a mast, but he did not mean to put this up till the raft was almost ready to launch. "It's easier to hide a flat raft with no mast, if that man pays us a visit too soon," he said.

"How can we hide it, though?" asked

Tom, looking at the heavy raft. "We really can't toss it into the heather as we could do with planks!"

Andy grinned. "We'll simply rig up the tent above it, and pile heather on the raft, which will then make the floor. I don't think anyone is likely to think that our tent is hiding a raft!"

In three days the raft was quite complete. Andy had decided to take all the food in the big wooden box in which the man had brought the tins and jars on his last visit.

"We can nail the box to the floor of the raft," said Andy, "and our food will stay there quite safely! If we put it loose on the deck of the raft, everything would get thrown off in a rough sea."

There came a warning cry from Pippa not long after that. She had seen a boat coming round the cliff on the far side of the cave-beach. Hastily the boys put up the tent over the raft, and Zoe strewed heather and bracken over the deck. She could not hide the box of food in the middle of the raft, however.

"Never mind about that," said Andy. "Just put a rug over it, and it will look like a seat or something."

There were two men this time, and one of them was the one who spoke English.

Andy went down to meet them. "Please, sir, won't you give us a boat to go home in?" he said to one, knowing perfectly well that the man would say no.

"No," said the man at once. "You will stay here for as long as we wish. But soon the winter will come, and a tent will be no good to you. Is there any building here that can be mended?"

"No," said Andy, who did not wish the man to examine the buildings, and perhaps ask where the tumbledown shack was. This had almost disappeared by now, for the children had taken all the planks for their raft!

"Let me see your tent," said the man. Andy's heart sank. It would be too bad if the raft was found just as it was finished. He took the man to the tent in silence.

The man looked inside. He saw the box in the middle covered with a rug. "What's that?" he asked.

"It's the box of food the man brought us the other day," said Andy, and he pulled off

the rug. The man saw at once that it was only a box of food and he nodded. He did not go inside the tent, luckily, or his nailed boot might have gone through the heathery covering and struck against the wooden raft below. Then he would certainly have pulled aside the heather and seen the children's secret.

Pippa and Zoe watched, very pale and scared. Tom sat nearby and whistled. The man still stood looking into the tent, and all the children felt very anxious indeed – and he said, "I will send men to put you up a rough hut for the winter. Be sensible children and you will be looked after – but if not, you will be very sorry for yourselves."

The children were very thankful indeed when they saw the boat with the two men in go off over the water. They heaved deep sighs of relief and looked at one another.

"Well, I think we're safe to make our escape soon now," said Andy. "I don't expect any men will be sent for a while. We'll drag the raft down to the shore early tomorrow morning, and I'll set up the mast and rig the sail as best I can. Then Tom and I will start off."

The girls did not like being left alone on the island, and yet they knew Andy was right. Somehow he must get home and tell the people there what they had discovered.

They all went to bed early that night, for tomorrow was to be an important day! And in the morning, early, they took down their tent, dragged off the heather that covered the raft, and tied ropes to it, to pull it down to the beach.

"Now we're off on another adventure!" said Andy, dragging the raft. "Heave-ho! Heave-ho! Down to the sea we go!"

CHAPTER TWENTY-TWO

Away on the Sea

The raft was dragged right down to the sea. In the middle of it Andy fixed the post that was to be the mast. He rigged up the old sail very cleverly. The box of food was firm below the mast – they had enough to last them for some days. They took a big tin of water with them too, but expected to use the juice of the tins of fruit to quench their thirst after they had drunk all the water.

Andy had made two rough paddles to help the boat along and to guide it. Zoe handed Tom the two warmest rugs to wrap themselves in at night, though Andy said they wouldn't be any use – they would get wet with the very first wave that splashed over the raft! But to please the girls he took the rugs.

"Andy, you can dry them in the sun in the daytime," said Pippa, "and you might be glad of them. We've got plenty here."

"Now don't worry," said Andy, jumping on to the raft. "You won't hear anything for days and days, because we've got to get back home, and then tell our tale and then ships have got to find their way here. So you'll have to wait a long time."

"What shall we say if the men want to know where *you* are?" asked Pippa anxiously.

"Just say we have disappeared," said Andy. "And if you like, do another bit of pretending and make a fuss!"

"All right," said Pippa. "Anyway, you may be quite sure we won't tell them you've gone on a raft."

"No, we don't want their seaplanes hunting the sea for us!" said Andy, letting the sail unfurl. "Now, goodbye and see you soon!"

Tom pushed out the raft and jumped up on it. He took a paddle and guided it. Andy let the sail billow out. The wind caught it and the little raft leaped along over the waves like a live thing!

The boys waved wildly to the girls. Little waves splashed over the deck of the raft and wetted the boys' legs. If they ran into a stormy sea they would soon be wet through, but at that moment they cared nothing for what might happen! They were very excited and very anxious to guide their little raft on the right course.

The sail flapped and billowed finely. Andy had rigged it most cleverly, and the wind shot the little craft along swiftly.

"Look out!" cried Andy. "There's a fat wave coming!"

The raft sailed into the wave – *slap!* It drenched Tom, and he laughed and shook himself like a dog. The sun was out and the boy's clothes soon dried.

The boys stood on the raft, holding on to the mast and looking back on the cluster of islands. They lay in the sea together, and

looked very small now that the boys were so far off. They could no longer see the girls. And soon even the islands too would disappear, then the boys would be quite alone on the wide sea.

"Do you really know which way to go, Andy?" said Tom.

"More or less," said Andy. "I can guide the raft by the sun in the daytime, and by the stars at night. It's a good thing for us that the wind is just in the right direction. I hope it lasts. It's easy enough now, but if the wind changes, things will be very difficult!"

Now the boys could no longer see any land at all. They were alone on the wide green sea. Below them the water was very very deep. The sea was not rough, but a little choppy, and the raft bobbed like a cork over the waves. Every now and again a wave hopped over the side and wetted the deck of the raft. The boys got used to this and didn't even move when a wave reared its head to run across the raft.

"Now," said Andy, as they sped through the water, "what about something to eat?"

They opened a tin of salmon and a tin of

pears, and had a good meal, though Tom longed for some bread with the salmon. It was odd sitting there eating on the bobbing raft, all by themselves in the midst of a wide, heaving sea.

The day seemed endless, but at last the sun slid down the sky and the sea turned from green to purple in the twilight.

"It's not so warm now," said Tom, taking his jersey down from the mast and putting it on.

"Tom, see if you can have a nap for a while," said Andy. "I don't think we ought both to sleep at once. The wind might change, or a storm might blow up – you sleep now and I'll have a nap later."

Tom wrapped himself in a rug and tried to go to sleep. Andy slipped a rope round his waist and tied him to the box in the middle.

"You might roll off the raft in the middle of the night," he said with a grin. "I shouldn't like to look round and find you gone, Tom!"

Tom lay on his back and looked up at the night sky. It was a clear night, with no moon and the stars shone brightly. Andy pointed out the North Star to Tom.

"That tells me we are still going in the right direction," said Andy. "At this rate we should sight the coast we're heading for in about three or four days."

"Oh, as long as that!" said Tom, hugely disappointed. "I thought we'd only be a day or two, going at this pace."

"This is a raft, not a sailing dinghy," said Andy. "Now go to sleep. I'll wake you if I need you for anything."

Andy woke Tom near dawn and told him to sit up and keep watch. "The wind's still right," he said. "Watch it, Tom. You can see the North Star, can't you? I'm so sleepy I can't keep awake much longer."

Andy tied himself up safely, lay down and was asleep as his head touched the rug that made a pillow for him.

Tom sat and watched the dawn coming. He wished he could wake Andy up so that he could see the magnificent sight too. There was nothing but sea and sky, all glowing with colour.

After a while Tom felt very hungry, but he waited till Andy woke up and they shared a tin of corned beef, with pineapple to follow. They poured water into the tin with the juice and made a kind of pineapple drink to have later on in the day.

Andy sniffed the wind, and looked at the sky. "There's a change coming," he said. "I do hope we won't be blown out of our way. We were getting on so well!"

The sea was rougher. Waves slopped over the deck almost every minute now. Only by sitting up on the box of food could the boys keep dry from the waist up. Once or twice the raft heeled over, and Tom had to clutch the mast to keep from overbalancing.

"Bother!" said Tom. "What does the sea want to get so rough for? It's a good thing we're both good sailors or we'd be very ill."

Andy looked anxiously at the sky. "I'm afraid the wind is changing," he said. "We shall be blown right out of our way if it does. I think we'd both better tie ourselves firmly to the mast. A big wave could easily dash one of us overboard!"

So they tied themselves to the mast, and then watched the scurrying clouds, wondering if they would suddenly slow down and fly the other way!

CHAPTER TWENTY-THREE

A Wonderful Surprise!

Alas for Tom and Andy! The wind did change and blew strongly the other way. Andy took down the sail hurriedly. "We don't want to be blown back to our island!" he said. "We must just bob along without a sail now and hope for the best. When the wind changes again we'll put up the sail once more."

"I wonder if they've found out that we've escaped," said Tom. "They might send a seaplane out after us if they've found out we've gone. They'd know we were on a raft."

"Well, the girls wouldn't give us away, that's certain," said Andy. "But the enemy might guess we'd made a raft, if they searched the island for us and missed us – and they could send out a seaplane or two to hunt the seas for us. We're a good way from the island now, but a seaplane could easily find us."

"I hope one doesn't," said Tom. "Isn't this wind frustrating, Andy? It just won't stop! It's wasting all our time."

The wind blew cold. The sun was behind the clouds. Big waves slapped around the raft and seemed really spiteful. "Almost as if they want to snatch us off," said Tom, tightening the rope that tied him safely to the mast. He shivered. There was no shelter at all on the open raft, and no way of getting warm or dry now that the sun was not to be seen.

And then, towards afternoon, the wind dropped again, and the sun shone! What a relief that was! The boys sunned themselves gladly, and were soon warm. Andy rigged the sail again. "We'll get the wind we want this evening," he said. "We'll be ready for it."

Sure enough, as the sun slid down the western sky, the wind got up again, and this time it was blowing from the right quarter! Andy was delighted.

The sail filled and the little raft raced along nobly. "I think the wind's set in properly now," said Andy, pleased. "If only it holds for another couple of days we may be home – or, at any rate, see a ship we can hail."

The wind became stiffer as the evening drew on. The sun was just about to slip over the skyline when Andy sat up straight and looked alarmed.

"Can you hear a noise?" he asked Tom.

"Plenty," said Tom. "The wind and the waves and the sail!"

"No, not that sort of noise," said Andy. "A noise like a seaplane!"

Tom's heart almost stopped beating. He sat and listened.

"Yes, there's a seaplane about somewhere," said Andy. "Bother! If it's really hunting for us it will be sure to find us. Just as we've got away so nicely, too!"

Tom went pale and looked up anxiously at the sky. Both boys could now hear the hum of the engines quite clearly.

And then the seaplane appeared, flying fairly low and quite slowly. It was plain that it was hunting the seas for something.

"Can we do anything, Andy?" said Tom.

"We'd better jump into the water, hold on to the raft, and hope that maybe the seaplane will think there's no one on it," said Andy. "Only our heads will show beside the raft, and they might not notice them. Come on, quick!"

The boys slid into the water over the side of the raft. They hung there with their hands, only their heads showing. They waited anxiously.

The great seaplane came zooming overhead, very close to the water. It had seen the raft and was coming to examine it more closely. How the boys hoped that when the raft was seen to be empty the seaplane would fly off!

The plane flew over the raft. It circled round and came back again, flying once more over the raft. It circled round again and then, to the boys' great dismay, it skimmed over the water and landed there, not very far off.

"It's no good, Tom. We're discovered," said Andy. "We may as well climb back on to the raft. Look, they're letting down a boat."

The boys climbed back on to the raft, angry and disappointed. And then Tom gave such a tremendous yell that Andy nearly fell overboard with fright.

"Andy! ANDY! Look at the sign on the seaplane! It's not the foreigners. It's British!"

Andy looked – and sure enough there were the familiar markings! And then such a change came over the boys. Instead of sitting there sullen and angry, they went completely mad. They stood up and danced on that rocking raft! They yelled, they waved, they stamped! And, as you can imagine, Tom lost his balance and fell right into the water.

Andy pulled him up, gasping and spluttering. "Oh, Andy, we're rescued! Suppose it had flown off and not come down to examine the raft!" And then Tom went mad again and shouted for joy.

The boat from the seaplane came nearer. It had two men in it, and they hailed the boys.

"Ahoy there! Where are you from?"

"Ahoy there!" yelled back Andy. "Ahoy there!" He was too excited to shout anything else.

The boat came alongside the raft and the men pulled the two boys into it.

"Why, it's only a couple of boys," said

one man. "How did you get here?"

"It's a long tale to tell," said Andy. "I think I'd better tell it to the chief, if you don't mind."

"All right. The commander's in the plane," said the first man. They rowed the boys off the seaplane, and left the little raft bobbing about on the sea alone. Tom was quite sorry to see it go. He had grown fond of it. He was sorry to think of the wasted food, too!

The boat reached the enormous seaplane. The boys were pushed up into it, and a grave-faced man turned to receive them.

And then Andy got a second shock, for Tom once more let out a yell that really scared him!

"DADDY! Oh, Dad! It's *you*!"

The grave-faced man stared at Tom as if he couldn't believe his eyes. Then he took the boy into his arms and gave him such a bear-like hug that Tom felt as if his bones would break!

"Tom! We've been hunting for you ever since we heard you'd gone off in that boat and hadn't come back!" he said. "Where are the girls – quick, tell me!"

"They're safe," said Tom. "We left them on the island. Oh, Dad, isn't this too good to be true! Dad, this is Andy. He's been such a star. We'd never have escaped if it hadn't been for him."

"What do you mean – *escaped*?" said Tom's father in surprise. "Escaped from what?"

"We've got a big secret to tell you," said Tom. "We've found out something interesting. You tell him, Andy."

"Well, sir," said Andy, "we got thrown off up the coast of some desolate islands where nobody lives now. There are foreigners using them as a base for submarines and seaplanes. There are caves stored with food, and there must be stores of fuel somewhere, too."

"What?" shouted Tom's father. He called his men near and they all listened to Andy's tale. The boy told it well.

"And we were just escaping on the raft we had made when we saw you," finished Andy. "We slipped over the side of the raft to hide – but you must have seen us."

"We didn't," said Tom's father. "But we were puzzled about the empty raft and came down to examine it. Little did we think you and Andy were there! This seaplane and two others have been scouring the seas about here looking for the boat you went off in. We were afraid you might be drifting about in it, half starving. Your poor mother has been dreadfully upset."

"Oh dear, I was afraid she would be,"

said Tom. "But, never mind, we're all safe, Dad – at least, I hope the girls are safe!"

"They will be, very soon," said the boy's father in a grim voice. "We shall rescue them – and clean up those submarines and seaplanes in no time! You've done a marvellous thing, Tom and Andy!"

"I hope my father won't be very angry with me for losing his boat," said Andy. "Though we might perhaps be able to get it back now."

"Your father won't be angry with you for anything once he sees you're safe, and hears the tale you've just told me!" said Tom's father. "Settle down now – we're going up."

"Back to the island to rescue the girls?" asked Tom eagerly. His father shook his head.

"No," he said. "They must wait, I'm afraid, till I get this news through. I'll send a message home that we've got you safe, and have got great news, but that's all. This is too important to be told to anyone but the chief himself."

CHAPTER TWENTY-FOUR

Return to the Islands

The seaplane took Tom and Andy back to headquarters, where Tom's father made his report, and handed Tom's camera in for the pictures to be developed. There was great excitement as everyone examined them.

Tom and Andy had been questioned closely. They told their story clearly and well, and the men who listened to them were amazed at the adventures the four children had been through.

"Well, you've stumbled on an astonishing secret," said one man who had been listening. "We'll be able to spring a real surprise on that base, and clean up all those submarines and seaplanes. Who knows what they were planning to do!"

"Please, sir, what about my sisters?" asked Tom anxiously. "Will you get them away before you do anything?"

The men laughed heartily. "Of course!"

said one. "That'll be our first job. We'll send your father's seaplane to rescue them, and after that – oho! A big surprise will come to those islands!"

"Come along," said Tom's father. "You and Andy must come with me to the islands so that you can tell me quickly where the girls are."

The boys were thrilled! To go off in that wonderful seaplane again – to the islands! And to rescue the two girls under the very noses of the foreigners! What fun!

They all went aboard the great seaplane. It rose from the surface as gracefully as a gull and soared up and round, then flew in a straight line towards the far-off islands.

"As soon as we sight the islands, we'll go cautiously," said Tom's father. "We don't want to warn the men if we can help it! You can guide us to the good landing-place off the shore of the second island, Andy. Then you and Tom and a couple of men can get to the first island and take off the girls. Then off we'll go again and give the signal for the Navy to go and surprise those foreigners!"

"Great!" cried the boys. "What a shock for them!"

"It's a shock they deserve," said Tom's father grimly. "We are sending three ships and some aeroplanes to deal with the submarines and seaplanes. So, you see, we want to get the girls off as quickly as possible."

The boys kept a watch for the islands, and as soon as they caught sight of them, lying flat in the sea, they both shouted loudly:

"There they are!"

"Which is the one the girls are on?" asked Tom's father eagerly.

"The first one," Tom said. "And the next one is where the food-cave is, and the third one is where the submarines are. I don't know anything about the other islands further off. We didn't have time to explore those."

"Well, *we* shall," said the boy's father, in a grim tone. "Now, Tom, we're almost on the coast of the second island. Is that the smooth bit of water we can land on, just down there?"

"Yes!" cried both boys, as they saw the flat stretch of water that lay between the reef of rocks and the cave-beach. The seaplane circled round and flew down gracefully.

"The tide's a bit too deep over the rocks that lead to the first island," said Tom in disappointment. "We can't climb over them to rescue the girls yet."

"We'll take a boat, then," said his father. "Are those the caves you hid in, Tom?"

"Yes, that one just there is the one that leads to the food-cave," said Tom. "Like to see it, Dad? You might find something of importance there, perhaps."

"Yes, we might as well have a look," said the boy's father.

So a boat shot off from the seaplane carrying the two boys, Tom's father, and two men. They landed on the beach and went towards the cave.

Tom led his father into the cave. "Look!" he said, "do you see all these boxes and chests, Dad? They're absolutely *full* of food of all sorts. I can tell you it came in handy when we were so hungry. At first I kept a list of the things we took, thinking that we would pay for them when we discovered the owner, but—"

Tom stopped. An odd noise was coming

from a big chest nearby. He stared in surprise. "What's that noise?" said Tom's father at once.

"There's something in that chest," said Tom in a trembling voice. "Is it the men playing a trick?"

"We'll soon see," said his father in a fierce voice. He rapped out an order to the two men with him, and they went over the chest. They ripped off the top – and everyone stood ready to fight.

But it was two small, excited, rather

grubby little girls who rose up from the chest, shouting loudly:

"Tom! Andy! It's us! We hid here because we thought you were the men and then we couldn't get the lid off again!"

Their father picked them out of the chest and hugged them.

"Daddy! It *is* you! However did you get here? Oh, you've come to rescue us just in time. What a good thing you came to the cave!"

"Why are you on *this* island?" asked the boys.

So Pippa and Zoe told their tale, their words tumbling over one another. They had spent a dull day when the boys had left, and had made themselves some cocoa to cheer themselves up before they went to bed.

"Then we heard the motor-boat come over from the other island, and were very frightened. We were sure that the men had discovered that the boys had gone," said Zoe.

"We were even more scared when two men came up to our tent," went on Pippa. "But we managed to get rid of them till the next day."

Then the men had come back and searched the island. When they couldn't find the boys, they realised that they must have escaped on a raft, and they threatened to take the girls away and to search the seas by seaplane for the boys.

"So," Pippa went on, "the next morning we climbed the rocks to this island. We decided to hide in the Round Cave because we thought no one would find us."

"We had a horrible night here, and it took us ages to get to sleep, so we didn't wake till we heard the seaplane come over. We thought the seaplane belonged to the men so we found this old chest to hide in, but we couldn't get the lid off, which was why we made such a noise! We'd heard Dad's voice and wanted some help!" Zoe finished off.

When their father heard that the men had guessed that the boys had left on a raft, he hustled them all out of the cave very quickly.

"We'll get back to our plane," he said. "We shall get into a spot of trouble if the men see us here. If they really think the boys have gone to tell their secret they'll be watching for us, though not expecting us quite so soon. Come along!"

They all rowed off to the seaplane. The girls were thrilled to get inside it, and even more excited when it rose into the air and left the sea far below.

The boys were looking down as the plane flew swiftly along. Suddenly Tom gave a shout.

"Ships! Look! Steaming below us at top speed! Are they going to the islands?"

"They are," said his father. "There will be quite a lot of noise round about your islands very soon! And, look – here are aeroplanes, too, to help the ships."

Several aeroplanes flew near the seaplane. The children felt tremendously excited. What a pity they had left before the fun began!

"And now, home we go to your mother," said the children's father, "and to Andy's father. Both will be so very glad to have you back again."

"But what will my father say about his lost fishing boat?" wondered poor Andy. "Whatever will he say?"

CHAPTER TWENTY-FIVE

The End of the Adventures

The seaplane flew over the water, and at last landed on the shores of the fishing village where Andy lived.

The little beach was soon crowded with people – fishermen and their wives, children, visitors – all shouting and cheering. The news had gone round that the four missing children had been found!

A boat set off to fetch the children from the plane. It was rowed by Andy's father! How Andy shouted to see him!

"Dad! We're back again!"

The children tumbled into the boat, all talking at once. Andy's father patted his boy on the shoulder and smiled at him out of eyes as blue as Andy's. Tom's father came with them. He had two days' leave and was going to spend it with his wife and children.

The people on the beach cheered and

shouted. The little boat was pulled up the shore by willing hands. And then the children saw their mother! They rushed to her and hugged her like bears, shouting and laughing.

"Now, now, give me a look in," said their father, smiling, and the whole family went up the beach together. Andy went off with his father. He had no mother, so he thought twice as much of his father.

What a talking and chattering there was that evening! Soon they were all washed and dressed in clean clothes. It felt nice to be tidy and fresh again. They hung round their mother and tried to tell her all their adventures at once.

"Andy was brilliant," said Tom. "We could never have done what we did if it hadn't been for him. The girls were pretty brave too – I was proud of them."

"And old Tom didn't do so badly, except that he left his precious camera behind and got us all into a fix!" said Pippa. "He was as brave as could be."

"Well, I'm proud of you all," said their mother, hugging them. "But oh, I was so awfully worried when you didn't come back. I sent a message to your father and he came in a seaplane and hunted for you for days. He wouldn't give up hunting – and it's a good thing he didn't, for he found you just in time! You and Andy would never, never have got home on that little raft, you know, Tom."

"Wouldn't we?" said Tom, surprised. "I thought perhaps we might."

"I don't think Andy thought there was much hope," said the children's father, "but he knew it was your only chance, and he knew, besides, that he had to try to tell someone what you had discovered. It means a lot to our country to know the secret of those desolate little islands."

There was a dull booming sound as the children's father finished speaking. Tom looked at his father.

"Is that guns?" he asked.

"Yes. It will be the end of those submarines," said his father gravely. "And I rather think that our aeroplanes will drive off any seaplanes round about those islands – those that are not destroyed will fly back to their own country!"

Andy came tearing up to the cottage. "I

say!" he yelled. "Do you hear the guns? I bet they're waking up the islands! What a shock for those men!"

"Andy, was your father angry about his fishing boat being lost?" asked Tom, who knew how much Andy was dreading what his father might say about that.

"He hasn't said a word about it," said Andy. "Not a word, except that we're going to fish with my uncle, now that we've lost our own boat. Maybe one day we'll save enough money to get a boat again."

"I wouldn't worry about that if I were you," said Tom's father unexpectedly. "I rather think there is a surprise coming for you tomorrow!"

"Oh, what?" cried all the children, and Andy stared at Tom's father in surprise.

"Wait and see," was the answer. So they had to wait – and the next day the surprise arrived!

Andy saw it first. He was on the beach, mending nets, and the other children were helping him. Andy happened to look up – and he saw a fishing boat rounding the corner of the cliff.

"Whose boat is that?" said Andy. "I

haven't seen it before! What a beauty! Look at its red sail!"

The children stood up and watched the little fishing boat drawing in to shore. It really was something, fresh with new paint, and with its red sail billowing out in the breeze.

It came to the beach and a man jumped out. He saw the children and hailed them. "Hi, give me a hand here!"

They ran to help. "Whose boat is this?" asked Tom.

"I've got to find the owner," said the man. "It's for the boy whose name has been given to the boat."

The children looked at the name on the boat. There, painted boldly, was Andy's own name – *ANDY*!

"*Andy*! The boat is called *Andy*!" squealed Pippa. "Oh, Andy, does that mean it's for you?"

Andy stared at the boatman in astonishment and joy. "It *can't* be for me!" he said.

"Well, if you're Andy, it's yours," said the boatman. "I understand that it's a little reward for services rendered; wasn't it you who discovered the secret of those islands, and lost your boat in doing so?"

"Wow!" said Andy, and could say no more. He stood and stared at the lovely boat in delight and pride. It was the finest in the bay. Never, never could Andy ever have saved enough money to buy a boat like this!

The other three children were full of joy. They had been so sorry for Andy when his boat had been lost, for they knew that he and his father earned their living from fishing. And now Andy had a much better boat! They danced and shouted and clapped Andy on the back till the boy almost fell over.

"You must share the boat with me," said Andy, suddenly finding his tongue again. "It'll belong to all of us!"

"Well, we have to go back to school again soon," said Tom, rather sadly. "But we're to come here for holidays always, Andy, so we can share it then. Can't we go out in it now?"

Many people had come down to the beach to look at the fine new fishing boat. Andy's father and uncle came running down, and when they heard the news they could not believe their ears!

"It's called *Andy*," said Tom proudly. "Isn't it a fine boat?"

Andy's father got into the boat and looked at it carefully. His blue eyes gleamed with joy. "Ah, Andy lad," he said, "this is a wonderful boat." And then Andy, his father, and the three children all got into the fishing boat that evening to make the first trip together.

"Now don't get lost on any more adventures!" shouted the children's father, who had come down to the beach to watch. "Just go fishing now, and bring me back something for breakfast! I don't want submarines and seaplanes this time!"

Everyone laughed and wished them good luck. The sail flapped happily, and the boat sped on like a live thing towards the fishing-grounds.

And there we will leave them all, scudding along in the *Andy* – and we'll say the same – good luck to you, Andy, and your red-sailed boat!